TransAtlantic Ties

KATHERINE GIRSCH

Published by Katherine Girsch
Salem, Oregon
United States of America

Cover Design: Bill Girsch

ISBN 978-0-57879-173-9
eBook 978-0-57879-174-6

Library of Congress Control Number: 2020921248

In memory of life on earth before 2020 and with hope for our future.

Contents

LONDON INTERLUDE

2008

September was a romantic low point for me. At the beginning of the month, I told Sarah, the woman I'd been seeing for eight weeks, that I wasn't ready for a committed relationship. An outright lie. Five years after a divorce had broken my heart, I was more than ready to commit again, just not with Sarah. As time passed, I seemed to make ever worse choices as I searched for a partner.

My friend Jack offered an opinion. "You're looking for the anti-Kate. That's a mistake. Even though your marriage to her didn't work out, she was in many ways your ideal woman—warm, kind, oblivious of her beauty. You're a Shakespeare-quoting sheep farmer turned Oxford scholar turned crusader for social justice." He paused for a breath, then continued holding forth. "You're quirky, for Christ's sake. Look for a woman who appreciates your eccentricity, who doesn't spend an hour in front of a mirror every morning and the rest of the day keeping score. Someone you can take up north to meet your family. These designer blondes you insist on seeing, however talented they may be, are not going to cut it."

Jack had a point, but I hadn't asked for his advice and was in no mood to take it. "I do want a woman who'll feel comfortable in Yorkshire. But who are you to give relationship advice? You're hardly a shining success. And what the hell is a 'designer blonde'?"

He refused to elaborate. "Don't pretend the aptness of that construction escapes you. You took bloody first-class honours in English Language and Literature. You've explicated far more obscure phrases."

I filed the term away in the back of my mind under the heading, "Jack Being Jack," and threw myself into my work. Spent a month organizing a symposium of voices from within the immigrant community to address challenges they faced in London. The press showed up on the morning of the conference. The men and women who spoke shared inspiring stories of courage and hope in the face of adversity. I was proud of them. Of myself.

But by the time I left South Kensington Station that afternoon, the warmth of my colleagues' praise had faded, and loneliness competed with my feeling of pride in the forum I'd put together. Peals of laughter spilled out onto the street through the open door of a hotel bar. I decided to drop in for a whiskey, maybe two, before heading to my silent flat.

I stepped from the glare of late afternoon sun into a cool dim space, and there she sat, a happy-looking woman in a light grey jacket and skinny black trousers—her hair all rippling, honey-colored waves—raising a champagne flute in a solitary toast. I crossed the room. *Here I go, another blonde.* Took a seat next to her and signaled the barman. "Jameson on the rocks."

Within minutes, I discovered the woman was an American widow toasting her husband and son, who'd died in an automobile accident. Not at all happy. "My parents-in-law held a celebration of life for the two of them last October. I could neither celebrate nor grieve. I didn't talk about either of them, not a word, for almost a year. Does that make me sound heartless?"

"No, I don't think so. Would you like to talk about them now?"

"Yes." She stared over my head, across the room. "My husband was a wonderful human being—joyful and calm and fearless—a kind of philosopher-scientist. And a nature lover. He and our son spent hours crawling on their hands and knees searching for life, in fields and woods and even"—a laugh bubbled up between her words—"in the cracks of Brooklyn's sidewalks."

A second later, tears filled her eyes. "Their last outing was to the family truck farm in the Finger Lakes of New York. One year ago today, my son called me from the car as they drove home to Brooklyn and told me about the pumpkins he'd picked for Halloween. I never heard his voice again." She wiped her cheeks with the back of her hand. "It's your turn to talk. Tell me about your family, your life."

"I grew up in the country, the Dales. My mum's a psychotherapist, and my dad's a literature teacher. My granddad was a shepherd. Psychology never captured me, but Shakespeare and sheep were in my blood, and I underwent a great internal tug of war before I finally abandoned my dream of farming and began reading literature at Oxford. As it happened, my struggle wasn't over. The cultural divide between North and South was wider than a Yorkshire farm boy could fathom." She listened—eyes fastened on me—as if hungry for every word. "Fortunately, I met Jack, quite a sophisticated London bloke, on the day I came up and he saw me through my rocky introduction to the politics of class. The two of us have been mates for over twenty years."

She gave an enthusiastic nod. "Oh yeah, I get that. Literature is in my DNA as well. The poetry of Shakespeare and Yeats above all. I grew up savoring their words in the Finger Lakes. At eighteen, I left home to study in New York City. The bus trip lasted just over six hours but carried me to a whole new realm. I was lost until I met Laura, a girl from the Bronx, who introduced me to that brave new world. Sixteen years have passed, and we're still friends."

I ordered us each another drink. We sat there in the bar exchanging alcohol-fueled stories for two hours. I silently congratulated myself on raising her spirits until one glass of wine too many for her and a request from me, "Tell me about the rest of your family—mum, dad, siblings," led to a confession.

Years before losing her husband and son, she'd lost her father, her mother, and her brother. "My little brother, who was going to be my friend forever. I tempted fate by naming my baby for him. I wanted him to become a man along with my son." The look on her face was as sad as any I'd ever seen. "But my son died when he was only five." Her voice cracked. "Everyone I love, everyone who loves me, dies. What kind of person does that happen to? What kind of person am I?" She ran outside and vomited.

Limp and tear-soaked, she walked with me to my flat. I handed her a towel and a pair of pajamas. "You should have a shower." She nodded. Ten minutes later, I tucked her up in my bed, folded the clothes she'd strewn about the bathroom, and pulled out the sofa for myself. However besotted I'd become over the course of the evening, I was not about to sleep with an inebriated, grieving widow.

The next morning, she walked into the kitchen dressed in her rumpled shirt and trousers. Looked me straight in the eye. "I am so embarrassed by my behavior, I hardly know what to say. As you probably surmised, I'm not much of a drinker. I can't even remember how I ended up in your flat." She paused and there was a catch in her voice. "We didn't sleep together, did we?"

"Right, we didn't. I slept in the living room." I took a mug from the cupboard and reached for the carafe. "You could use a coffee."

"No, no." She was adamant. "I've already stayed too long. Thank you though. So much. As I said, my memory of last night is limited, but I do remember you were kind. You listened. You offered me your bed." She pressed her lips together. "God, I must have been pathetic."

"Not a bit of it. Apart from being sick quite close to a couple of front doorways, your behavior was impeccable."

She scoffed and walked down the entry hall. "I truly apologize for causing such an inconvenience." She took her jacket from the peg, sniffed it and shook her head in distaste. "I recall getting off the tube at South Kensington Station yesterday. Is it nearby?"

"It is. Out the door to the left and left again at the corner. Then straight ahead. You'll see it."

She put on her jacket and gave a little wave. She was about to walk out of my life. I couldn't let that happen. "I'd like your phone number. In case you've left something behind."

She didn't hesitate. "Oh, yeah. It's a U.S. number, 718-632-1824."

I pulled out my phone. "Would you repeat that? A bit more slowly?"

"Sure."

A minute later, she stepped out into the bright Saturday morning wearing her vomit-stained jacket. She was a lovely mystery. I didn't know what had brought her to London or how long she'd be staying. I watched her walk away. Her sleep-tousled hair bounced and glinted in the sun as she nodded at passing strangers. She reached the corner. Turned left and disappeared. I looked at her number in my contacts and laughed. We hadn't even exchanged names. *We'll have to introduce ourselves when I call her this afternoon. We can make a plan to talk together without alcoholic enhancement. I think I'll invite her up north to meet my family.* I had a lot to learn about her. But I was certain of one thing—she wasn't a designer blonde.

A TALK ABOUT LIFE

1945

Morning sun splashed the furnishings of Nell O'Neal's Brooklyn bedroom—an iron bed with a white coverlet, a maple blanket chest, and a black Singer sewing machine adorned with gold acanthus leaves. Against one wall, on a chest of drawers painted pale green, three photos formed a small altar. At its center in a tarnished frame, was a sepia-toned portrait of Nell, a slender bride whose light hair was crowned with a wreath of lily of the valley, standing beside Emmet, her handsome, dark-haired groom. Hand-colored photos of their two sons flanked the portrait—one, a decade old, of Johnny in Dublin, and the other of Jimmy, taken two years ago in a Brooklyn studio.

She walked across the room and contemplated the faces on the photos. Each boy's, her husband's, and finally her own, the face of an eighteen-year-old standing on the brink of her life to come, bursting with a joy she'd feared she might never feel.

◆

The year she was thirteen, Nell had spent the entire summer in bed with rheumatic fever. She would gaze with envy at her sister Nora's dimples and dark ringlets, her dancing energy. Their mother's words of sympathy, "Poor, sweet child, such a thin face and nary a wave in your hair," made Nell feel pitiful, and Mam's feeble attempt at optimism, "It's a blessing your fingers are nimble. You'll make a good wife one day," only exacerbated her melancholy. She gradually recovered her strength but continued to lament her thin face and limp hair.

It wasn't until she was seventeen that she came to believe straight, pale red hair and a slender face could be beautiful. Emmet O'Neal showed her the print of an Italian Madonna hanging in his mam's bedroom. "You see, Nell, she looks like you." He bought her a green hair ribbon. "Tie it on," he said. "It matches your eyes."

Her mam was hopeful for the first time in years. "That O'Neal boy has brought something out in our girl. She's got a spring in her step and a bit of color showing in her cheek."

◆

Now a widow of thirty-eight, Nell carried herself with dignity. Emmet had died in the Dublin bombing of 1941, and the next year she sailed from Ireland to New York with their two sons. Her mother had been correct about the deftness of her hands. She quickly became known as the finest seamstress in her Brooklyn neighborhood, able to fashion everything from sturdy snowsuits to exquisite wedding gowns, and had built up a nest egg over the past three years.

She was a confident woman, comfortable in her own skin, but the physical residue of rheumatic fever hung on, extracting a toll on her heart. She'd confronted many a challenge in her life, but today's task—preparing her son Johnny to parent his brother—filled her with trepidation.

Nell folded and refolded the fabric lying across a table, rearranged the contents of a small wooden sewing basket, and straightened the doily on the back of a burgundy mohair chair. Each action unnecessary. She was fidgeting. She glanced at the clock. Almost nine. *Johnny's shift will be ending.* Four loud knocks cracked the stillness. *That will be Jimmy. Not yet five years, but he knows to respect a closed door.*

She opened it and looked down at her son—his dark curls sleep-tangled, his blue eyes bright with anticipation for whatever the day might offer. He was the picture of Emmet, the father he'd never met. Both her boys were. "Mam, I slept long, didn't I?"

"You did. And you're all dressed and ready for breakfast, aren't you?"

"No. I'm all ready for Johnny." He took her hand and led her downstairs to the kitchen. "I ate cereal, and I washed my bowl and glass."

"Darling, when Johnny gets here, he and I are going to talk for a while. You can build with blocks or play with your fire truck until we've finished."

"No. I want to talk with you."

Nell shook her head. "Not today. We're going to close the door and have grown-up talk while you play down here in the kitchen."

His little shoulders drooped. He dropped his head momentarily, then looked up with a smile. "It's okay, Mam. But don't talk long or Johnny will get too tired to play."

She draped her arm around him. "We'll keep our conversation as short as possible. He'll not be too tired to play."

The morning games her two sons shared were sacred to Johnny. No matter how exhausted he might be after his shift at the firehouse, he spent time with the little boy—telling him stories, roughhousing, playing ball. More than a big brother, he was a father figure. Just fifteen when his dad died, Johnny had taken his overwhelming sadness and—with love and grace—transformed it into stories for Jimmy. Early on, Nell worried that he made Emmet too grand, but she came to appreciate the tall tales. Johnny was preserving the best of his father for himself as well as for his brother.

Jimmy's bright voice interrupted her musing. "I can wait on the stoop, though. So I'll see Johnny first. Right, Mam?"

"Right. You can send him on up to my room."

Five minutes later, Johnny rounded the corner and watched his little brother leap down the stairs and dash toward him. "You're in a right hurry today, Jimmy."

"I am. I need your help before you go in for your talk with Mam." He pointed to the adjoining house. "Up there, right on top of the light. See, it's a bird nest. Mick saw the eggs when the mother flew away yesterday. He says they're blue. She's gone again, but she'll be back in a minute. If we're quick, I can ride on your back and look inside, okay?"

"Up you go then." Johnny hoisted the feather-light boy onto his shoulders and strode toward the nest. One quiet peek, and they walked hand in hand back to their stoop.

Jimmy marveled, "The eggs really are blue." He looked up at his brother. "I hope your talk with Mam isn't too long."

"Yeah, right, me too." He patted his brother's back and started up the stairs to her room.

Through the open door, he could see Nell, tall and stately, looking out onto the street. *She's so beautiful. And she's strong.* She turned to him and he shook his head. "Mam, you know I don't want to have this conversation. It's not necessary. You can't give up. It's not right." He stopped abruptly. *I'm lecturing her. This meeting is supposed to be her chance to talk.*

She smoothed her skirt. *She's nervous.* It broke his heart to see her that way. *My dear mam. She doesn't want to have this talk any more than I do. She's doing her job, the way she always has.*

He remembered his dad's funeral. How she had held him tight, then grabbed his shoulders and pushed him back and faced him, her eyes brimming with tears. "We're a team," she'd said, as she patted her belly. "You and I and this little baby. Let's do Emmet proud." She had taken his arm as if he were a man, and they'd walked down the aisle together.

Nell ran her hands over her skirt again and walked across the room. "Oh, Johnny, your collar is fraying. Take off your shirt; I'll turn it while we talk."

He smiled and undid the buttons. "That's my mam. Never wastes a minute."

Sewing was second nature to Nell. The task seemed to relax her. "Johnny, I know this is a hard conversation. For both of us. But let's make it positive."

"You're going to talk about your death and make it positive." He scoffed. "I can't see how that's going to happen."

"Firstly," she said as she unpicked the collar, "I'm not about to die next week, but I want to speak my piece in a timely way. Secondly, it's to be a talk about life, not death. Do you understand?"

"Not yet. But keep talking. Maybe I will."

"You should know I've saved a tidy sum. I'll leave a nice little inheritance for the two of you."

"For feck's sake, Mam. I don't care about the money."

"Oh, darling, I know. It's my leaving you and Jimmy alone that concerns you. And that's what I want to talk about—what it's like to be a parent." Her eyes filled with tears, but her voice was resolute. "Parenting a child expands your heart. It's a joy, caring for him, watching him grow. Oh, but it's a burden and a trial as well. You think the hard part is going to be giving up your free time. Comforting a sick child throughout a night. Having a young one always hanging on your skirt." She chuckled. "That would be your pant leg.

"But that's not the real challenge. The predicament is knowing when to stand your ground. You can be pulled so hard. You want to give in, allow the child a little pleasure, save him a bit of hardship. Sometimes you know what's right, but it pains you to remain steadfast. Other times, it's difficult to determine the correct path, and even more so to carry through, but a parent has to."

"And that's what you're doing now, right?"

"Yes, I am. For you, learning to parent is going to be different from what it was for me. And more difficult. We have to be honest. You and Jimmy will have suffered a loss. We both know what that's like, but I had Emmet for sixteen years. He and I supported each other, learned together how to be parents. And truth be told, you were almost an adult when he died. I leaned on you, probably more than I should have." She wiped her eyes and studied the collar.

"You were the best mam a boy could have. Your leaning on me made me a man."

"And you are a good man, a responsible man. I couldn't leave Jimmy in better hands. But there's a catch. You're young; you have a life of your own to live. So when you're deciding what's good for your brother, making hard decisions for his sake, you're going to have to stop and ask, 'What's good for me?' And that's going to be a torment. To weigh out when a sacrifice is right and when it might be too much. As I said, most of parenting is joyful, but I don't envy you that part. I don't believe I could have carried it off on my own." She looked up from her work with a laugh. "But then, I didn't have a mam quite like myself to coach me."

She sewed one last stitch and began removing pins. "That's why we're having this discussion, one-sided though it may be. I'm giving you food for thought. God willing, I'll be on earth for a good while longer. I'm not saying goodbye yet. Today is a preview, a sort of prologue. Our conversation will continue. Next time it'll be your turn to talk; I expect you'll cry and rage at me. You can ask me any question you wish, and I'll answer with all the truth I have within me."

Nell held up the shirt. "Now doesn't it look fine? Almost like new. You put it on and run down and play with Jimmy while you're still wide awake."

He buttoned it as he walked to the door, then stood watching in admiration as his mother hurried across the room and took a rose-colored silk dress from a padded hanger. Oblivious of him, she murmured, "Such a lovely thing," then chided herself, "Best not waste time exulting in my creation. Rosemary Prendevel will be here to pick it up within the hour, and I've got twelve covered buttons to sew on." She turned back toward her worktable and started at the sight of Johnny in the doorway. "What? You're still here? Considering me with such a tender look?" She dismissed him with a smile and a wave. "Off with you. Jimmy will be waiting to play. We all have a lot of living to do."

DOING MAM PROUD

1958

Eight o'clock, Saturday morning. Johnny O'Neal—starting the first day of a seventy-two-hour leave—sat at his kitchen table with a second cup of coffee. He'd been a Brooklyn firefighter since 1944. Had long since adapted to the FDNY's shift schedule. He awoke each day, on the clock or off, grateful to be alive. He knew about death. Had lost his dad at fifteen, his mam before he turned twenty. And about life. He'd spent the last thirteen years parenting his brother, Jimmy. *I've done a decent job. Never had a really carefree day, but it's been worth the effort.* With his brother in his last year of high school, the hard part was over for Johnny. No more playing the heavy over homework. No more trips to the principal's office. Jimmy would graduate in a few weeks, work full time repairing boats throughout the summer, and start Brooklyn College in the fall. It was what their mother would have wanted.

Seven o'clock, Saturday evening. Jimmy O'Neal—tired, but exhilarated—left the marine maintenance shop where he'd just put in eleven hours and walked along 32nd Avenue toward home. That afternoon, he'd started rebuilding an inboard. He was crazy about working on engines. The only thing he liked as much was actually taking a boat out on the water. A grateful customer had invited him to spend last Sunday afternoon on his walkaround, had let him take the helm, and he was still glowing from the owner's praise, "You're a natural."

His older brother, Johnny, could fix anything electrical or mechanical, could hit a home run, catch a line drive. Jimmy wasn't sure he'd ever match those skills, but learning to rebuild an engine had granted him a sense of personal pride. *Someday I'll run a shop. Have a boat of my own.*

Half an hour later he bounded up the front stairs of the wood-frame house he shared with his brother and called through the screen door, "Hey, I'm home. What's up?"

"Not much," Johnny answered. "Spent the last two hours unplugging the bathroom drain and replacing a faucet. I'm about to step into the shower. I left a five-dollar bill on the coffee table. You can run out and pick us up a large pie."

Jimmy splashed his face with cold water at the kitchen sink and took off for Luca's. At the hole-in-the-wall pizzeria, "Book of Love" blared from the radio. He knew every word and sang along absently, but his mind was on an idea that had been playing in his head the past few days. He handed the cashier the five and declined the change. "You keep it." Was out the door and back home in a flash.

He laid the open pizza box in the center of the kitchen table, pulled two ginger ales from the fridge, and set out plates. He radiated enthusiasm, was bursting to share his plan. He brushed away all doubts about his brother's possible negative reaction. *I'll convince him. That's all there is to it.*

Johnny, his hair damp from the shower, walked into the kitchen and sat down. "How was your day?"

"Outstanding. I'm rebuilding an engine. God, I love working at the shop. Better than anything I've done in my life."

"Yeah, that's good." Johnny folded a slice of pizza and took a bite. "And you'll get forty hours a week starting in June. You're lucky to have a job you love."

"Yeah. You know, I'm thinking it's going to be more than a summer job. Tony says I can stay on this fall. He can use me full time."

"Saturdays would be great, but you can't work full time while you're in college."

In an instant, Jimmy's tone went serious. "That's something I need to talk to you about—I want to work full time. I'm not so interested in college. I'm not sure it's right for me."

Johnny laid his half-eaten slice on the plate. "You're not sure? I'm sure. You're seventeen years old. It's not up to you," he thundered. "You've got the grades. I've been saving for this ever since Mam died. It's what she wanted. It's what Dad would have wanted."

Jimmy shouted back, "Did you ever consider asking me what I wanted?"

"A parent doesn't ask a kid if he'd rather eat healthy food or candy. The kid can't make that kind of decision."

"Well, I don't have a parent, do I?"

Johnny swallowed. "I do my best."

Chastened, Jimmy lowered his voice. "You used a bad example. Eating candy and working a full time job aren't the same at all. Anyway, you didn't go to college. You turned out pretty good."

"Pretty good's not that great." He stood up and shook a finger at his brother. "Let me tell you something. I'll tell you why I didn't go to college. Here's why. I turned sixteen the year we moved from Ireland. It was real hard making the change from Dublin to Brooklyn at that age. On top of everything, I worked twenty hours a week during my last two years of high school. I barely made the grades to graduate. Besides, we didn't have money for college. I worked because I had to, not because it was fun." He put his uneaten pizza in the refrigerator. "I'm going upstairs to listen to the game."

Alone in the kitchen, Jimmy finished eating and washed his plate. *I told Johnny I didn't have a parent. That was low.* His brother's quiet response, "I do my best," had shamed him. He knew it was true, and Johnny's best was really good. He remembered the years of stories, the ball games. All the nights he'd spent crying in his brother's bed after Mam died. For the first time in his life, he thought about the fun Johnny might have missed by having to be a parent before he was twenty years old. It had never crossed his mind that being a firefighter might not have been his brother's first choice for a job. He switched off the kitchen light. *I want to work full time next fall. I am not going to college, but I won't yell about it. If Johnny needs to yell, that's okay. I'll be polite.*

Upstairs, Johnny turned off the radio and lay considering the words he'd spoken at the table. They were true. Their mam's fondest dream was college for Jimmy. She had set aside a portion of each week's income for his education. *The words might've been true, but I said them wrong. I was too harsh with him. I'm not the only one who's had a hard life. The kid never knew his dad. He lost his mother when he was four years old.* Johnny rolled over. *And all he had to take their place was a bumbling nineteen-year-old. I'll see that he goes to college, but I won't yell about it.* He remembered their mother's grace. *I'll never match that, but I can be tactful.*

Sunday morning, nine o'clock. Breakfast was special. Johnny had made pancakes with blueberry syrup and fried eggs with bacon and hash browns. Squeezed oranges for fresh juice. He loaded a stack of 45s—The Coasters, Dion and the Belmonts, The Monotones, and Paul Anka—on the record changer. They'd sing along while they ate.

"I want to apologize for last night. I got a little hot under the collar." He set the heaping platter of food on the table. "I made it sound like I resent not having gone to college, and I don't. When I said you were lucky to have a job you love, I knew exactly what I was talking about because I have one. I love my work and I love being your parent."

Jimmy's reply was heartfelt. "I was pretty rude myself. I'm sorry about saying I didn't have a parent. I do, and you're first-rate. Mam and Dad would be proud of you. But I meant what I said. I want to work on engines."

"I did a little thinking before you got up this morning," Johnny said. "I don't know much about college, but I know a person can study engineering. Might give you a leg up on understanding mechanics. Who knows? Maybe you'll invent some new kind of engine. Here's my deal. I am the parent, and I say you will go to college next fall. You can keep working on Saturdays, but you have to give college a go. Make good grades for a year. Then if you want to quit and go to work full time, you'll have my blessing."

"You're saying I don't have a choice."

"Nope. I'm saying you do have a choice, but you can't make it until you know the plusses and minuses of each option. If you're honest, you'll agree it's a fair plan."

Jimmy sat staring at the floor. "Okay, it's a deal," he said without looking up. At last, he raised his head and met his brother's eyes. "You knew Mam really well, didn't you?"

"Yeah, yeah. I did."

"And you're trying to do what she would've done, aren't you?"

"Yes, I am. But I can't do it alone. I need your help. Together, we're gonna do her proud." A record dropped—the Coasters' "Yakety Yak." Johnny pointed a finger at the hi-fi. "Now that's a family with problems."

CITY GIRL

1965

C arolyn, finishing the second year of a postgraduate programme in psychology at University of London, spent her days minutes from the city's mod epicentre. She had the glossy hair and expertly lined eyes of a swinging 60s girl, but she wasn't part of the scene. The intricacy of the human mind was more exciting to her than avant-garde music and art. When she looked toward the future, she knew what she wanted—a career as a psychotherapist. Still, at times she wondered if her present life wasn't a bit too serious.

The second week of June, Annabelle Cameron, a free-spirited exception to the average swotty psychology student, called and invited her to a midsummer bash. She accepted. *I need a little fun in my life. If I let London's celebration pass me by, I'll regret it someday.*

That's how she ended up in a noisy Mayfair flat listening to Geoffrey, one of Annabelle's sleek, entitled friends. He paused mid-sentence and looked directly into her eyes. *Uh-oh, here it comes.* Since Jean Shrimpton's appearance on the cover of *Vogue*, half a dozen men had asked her if she realized how much she looked like the model. At first she'd been amused. *I'm a tall, fair, blue-eyed brunette who wears black eyeliner and mini skirts. I look like hundreds of other London girls.* Then, annoyed. *It's a lazy way to carry on a conversation.* Finally, she was just bored. Since she couldn't change her height and wasn't about to abandon her makeup and short skirts, she put up with the comments. She knew exactly what Geoffrey was about to say.

"Has anyone ever mentioned how much you look like-" The look on her face stopped him. He continued a little sheepishly, "I was about to say 'that fashion model who's all the rage,' but of course you've heard it before." Carolyn rolled her eyes.

"And you're rather tired of it, right?"

"You're quite perceptive."

———

He called her the following Thursday. "Carolyn, it's Geoffrey. From the midsummer party. Annabelle gave me your number. I was wondering if you might like to come out with me for Indian food some evening."

Two days later they sat talking over lamb kabab and masala prawns. "I grew up in Primrose Hill," Carolyn said. "My mum is a proper English wife who keeps an immaculate house. My dad is a dealmaking barrister's clerk."

"A barrister's clerk? I begin my pupillage in September. It would be interesting to hear his side of the story."

"I don't think you'd enjoy his take on barristers. He's quite plain-spoken."

"From what I've heard, the good clerks always are."

"You're what my dad would call a toff."

"Ha. I imagine he would."

"But I take it you're open-minded." She cocked her head to one side. "Annabelle wouldn't have invited a stuffy, upper-class bore to her party."

"And I take it you're a bit closed-minded regarding class distinction." They both laughed, and he said, "I think we'll get on."

They did. Although the two of them spent most of their summer holiday hours reading and writing, the transformation of the city set a tone for their free time. They saw the latest films, went to parties where music drowned out conversation, and slept together. No talk of love. No romance. It was the change Carolyn had been looking for.

In August, Geoffrey procured two tickets to a Royal Shakespeare Company hit. "Quite a modern take on Hamlet," he told her. "Presents him as a contemporary youth disillusioned by the world. The reviews have been excellent."

Traffic on the M40 was heavy, and they arrived at the theatre with only moments to spare. Geoffrey led as they made their way to the exact center of the third row, excusing themselves as they passed in front of seated patrons. Carolyn stepped round a dark-haired man who gave a polite nod as she took the seat beside him. The performance was entertaining, not at all what she'd envisioned when she read the play at school, but it was the man on her left who caught her attention. Young and good-looking, he sat forward in his seat, apparently caught up in Hamlet's pain, but chuckling now and then at a line whose humour seemed to escape the rest of the audience. At the interval, she turned and reached out her hand. "I'm Carolyn. You seem to have a special connection with this play."

"I do. It's my favorite," he said, and they carried on talking. He taught literature at an independent girls' school in Yorkshire and traveled south to take in theatre offerings a couple of times a year. He hoped watching this modern production of *Hamlet* would inspire his teaching.

Geoffrey tapped Carolyn's shoulder. "I don't wish to break up your conversation, but perhaps we could all step out for some air."

"Oh, of course, we should." She touched the young man's forearm. "I'm sorry, I didn't get your name."

"I'm Gregory Bonham. Greg." The men shook hands, and they all walked out under the rose-streaked sky. Greg asked about the current London scene, and Carolyn and Geoffrey filled him in on the city's metamorphosis from grey and outmoded to bright and up-to-date. "You really should travel up to London and see for yourself," Geoffrey said as they headed back inside for another hour and a half of *Hamlet*.

Autumn came and went. Then Christmas holidays. Though Geoffrey, halfway through his pupillage, was overtaxed and Carolyn was absorbed in revision, they met for the odd tea or coffee, spent Sunday afternoons and a couple of nights together each week. Offered one another a respite from the stress of daily life. *We're good for each other*, Carolyn thought.

At the end of January, she discovered a letter from Leeds among her departmental notices.

22 January, 1966

Dear Carolyn,

I'm Greg, the man you sat next to at Hamlet last summer. You mentioned your postgraduate programme at University of London. A mate of mine who's a lecturer there obtained your office address for me. My half-term holiday begins in two weeks, and I have tickets to see an English translation of *A Flea in Her Ear* at the National Theatre on the second Thursday in February. It's one of the great French farces. Should be a brilliant production. I'd enjoy having you as my guest.

If the outing is not of interest to you, just ignore this invitation. I'll not be offended. However, if you are interested, contact me at High Green Hill, Chapman Bridge, Harrogate, HG3 7JE, UK.

Best regards,

Gregory Bonham

Carolyn set the note on her desk, looked at the ceiling, and tried to sort her feelings. She was less surprised by the fact that a man she scarcely knew had searched her out and invited her to join him than she was by her reaction. At that moment, the idea of spending an evening with Gregory Bonham was more appealing than anything else she could imagine.

A letter and a call settled it. They would meet at Waterloo Station on the tenth of February. She'd have to tell Geoffrey. *Tell him what?* Each of them socialized with members of the opposite sex. All platonic. This felt different.

A week later Carolyn broke the news to him while spreading clotted cream across a scone. "You remember the man from Yorkshire we met at *Hamlet* last summer?" She slipped her words in between bites. "He's going to be in the city this Thursday. He's invited me to see a play with him."

"Really? That's rather odd. Coming out of the blue like that. Perhaps it's a Yorkshire thing."

"Maybe," she replied. But she didn't think it was. She sensed it was something else. She wasn't sure what.

◆

She met Greg at four thirty on the day of the performance. Over fish and chips he told her about growing up in the Dales. He'd worked on his family's sheep farm until he left for university at seventeen. Though he traveled only as far as Leeds, the act changed his life. He moved back to the country after completing a postgraduate programme in literature, but he left farming behind. "While I was away, my parents moved to a small cottage on the far side of their property. I inherited the large one I grew up in. I teach school during the week, and on weekends and holidays I work on my seventeenth century house. Reglaze windows and refinish floors. Mend stone walls. Someday I'll raise a family there."

The openness of his last statement gave Carolyn pause. She wanted to respond with something as personal, but she couldn't think what it might be. "Last summer was the first Shakespeare performance I'd seen. My family's not at all cultured, and my literary education was rather inadequate. I did the reading assigned me, but Christmas Pantomime was all I knew of live theatre."

Greg smiled and inquired about her plans for the future. How she would use her postgraduate degree in psychology. Somehow, neither Geoffrey nor her parents had ever asked.

"I want to be a psychotherapist. Help people explore their minds."

"Will you set up a private practice?"

"Oh, no. I think joining an established clinic will be the best route for me."

"In London?"

"I imagine so. I've lived here my whole life. I'm a city girl."

"And the man you were with in Stratford-upon-Avon? . . . Is he still in the picture?"

"Yes . . . he is." Greg scrutinized her face but said nothing. Although the silence was awkward, Carolyn was happy he had no more questions. She was out of answers.

He looked at his watch. "We'd best set out. Good to arrive early when you have center seats."

They walked the six blocks to the theatre without speaking. The silence was no longer awkward. *He's so calm.* His tranquility muted the roar of the city.

After the play, they headed back to Waterloo Station. "Was the evening all you expected?" she asked.

His dark eyes shone with pleasure. "Oh, even better. A marvelous romp. That Albert Finney was fantastic. What did you think?"

His reply wasn't quite what she'd been hoping for, but she smiled. "I agree. I've had a lovely time. Thank you."

He shook her hand. "You have my address and telephone number. Get in touch if you wish."

An hour later, she stood brushing her teeth. *It was a delightful evening. Why do I feel so sad?* She had a cry in bed thinking about Greg's last words. He was not going to call her, and she wouldn't contact him. They would never see each other again. The evening had been almost magical. She wiped her eyes. *It was a whim, a little break from ordinary life. Tomorrow I'll be back at work.*

She met Geoffrey for coffee the next morning. "How was your evening with the Yorkshireman?"

"Very nice. The show was exceptional. Albert Finney played the lead."

"Mmm. Where did eat dinner?"

"We had fish and chips."

"Ha. Is that a Yorkshireman's idea of an exciting pre-theatre meal?"

"It was my idea; it wasn't meant to be exciting. It was close to the theatre. And you needn't carry on calling him a Yorkshireman. His name is Greg. He's a lovely, literate man. He speaks French."

"Hmph. But he is from Yorkshire. As I recall, he dressed like a Yorkshireman, and he apparently hasn't the slightest notion of social conventions. Tracked you down and put you on the spot with his invitation."

"He didn't put me on the spot. I accepted because I remembered him as an interesting person." She raised her voice. "It's rude of you to disparage him."

"Sorry, I was just having a bit of fun. Incidentally, the man may speak French, but he speaks English like a Yorkshireman."

"He does, and my way of speaking isn't quite like yours. Does that offend you?"

"Not in the least. You have a charming London accent, which I adore."

He's jealous, she thought as they walked out of the cafe. *I had a brilliant evening with a person he doesn't know. I might feel the same if I were in his position.*

A week later, Geoffrey announced he'd had a call from Charlotte, an old friend who was visiting her parents in Surrey. "We were at Oxford together. She married an American. Divorced him within a year but stayed on in New York City. I'm meeting her for lunch at Brown's Hotel on Sunday. Hope you don't mind."

Carolyn and Geoffrey typically met for Sunday lunch. It occurred to her that his plan might be payback for her dinner with Greg, but she dismissed the notion. She knew Geoffrey's worldview. *Eating fish and chips with a teacher from Yorkshire is in no way comparable to lunch at an exclusive restaurant with one of his posh friends.*

To her surprise, she wasn't even slightly jealous. The solitary Sunday was a luxury. She left her reading and walked out into the early spring sunshine. Let her mind wander as she ambled from Shepherd's Bush to Parsons Green and back. Thought about her life. She reflected on the relationship with Geoffrey. *What's the point? What are we doing together?*

The following day, Geoffrey was full of praise for Charlotte's cleverness and style. "She's moving back to London next month. Will make some lucky man a brilliant wife."

"Really? I'm sure she doesn't speak the way I do. Her pronunciation is probably perfect for a barrister's wife."

He laughed. "I detect some jealousy and perhaps a touch of disdain for the upper classes that I noted at our first dinner together."

"As a matter of fact, I'm neither jealous nor disdainful, but I've come to a realization." Her next words poured forth unbidden. "Despite having grown up ten minutes from The Regent's Park, I'll always be the daughter of a proud clerk from Essex. No doubt I could affect the right accent, but I'm not cut out for your world, Geoffrey." She took a quick breath. "Thank you for a lovely year."

"You're saying goodbye." He sounded surprised, but not in the least disappointed. "Just like that? You're saying goodbye?"

Astonished at her spontaneous outburst and stung by Geoffrey's nonchalance, she stood flustered and silent until clarity arrived. The truth was obvious. "One of us has to."

"Quite right." He nodded. "But I will miss you."

She walked away pondering the exchange. Once again she asked herself, *Whatever were we doing together?*

Later that day, she collected her extra toothbrush and the few articles of clothing she'd kept in his flat. Left him her key and a note.

Dear Geoffrey,

Thank you for the past months. I'll not forget you. Since my flat is less than a mile from yours, we'll likely see each other from time to time.

Carolyn

The goodbye freed up space in her Sunday afternoons and in her life. Walking, which had been solely a means of hurrying from one spot to another, became an end in itself. She experienced London's spring—boisterous golden sprays of forsythia, clumps of daffodils, the filigree of redbud branches against a pale sky. Fragrances floated on the breeze. Daphne in April, lilac in May. *I've neglected this aspect of myself for years.* Her walks, coupled with the psychotherapy sessions required by her programme, opened sensual and psychic pathways to her very core. Her attitude toward coursework changed. The theoretical had become personal.

She didn't regret the months with Geoffrey. London's transformation had loosened society's rules, temporarily blurring the boundaries between classes, and the two of them enjoyed the benefits. *Each of us was a placeholder in the other's life. We were good for each other for a while.* She didn't know what their time together had meant to him, but for her the relationship and the goodbye had been a watershed. She was ready for the future.

———

June arrived. *No fabulous midsummer bash for me this year,* Carolyn thought. *I've never really been a party girl.* She passed the twilight of the year's longest day reading. No noisy revelers. No small talk. Just peace.

On the last Friday of the month, a letter from Gregory Bonham arrived in the afternoon post.

Dear Carolyn,

These summer days—when the sun sets late and each evening's long blue twilight verges on the next day's dawn—have set me to reading Yeats. His themes of friendship, love, and loss evoke thoughts of you, a woman with whom I've passed mere hours.

I asked you to contact me if you wished, and you haven't done. My head tells me to let you go. My heart says, "Give her another chance." If you're not interested in further interaction, you needn't respond. I'll not pursue you.

You have my address and telephone number.

Greg

Carolyn didn't hesitate. She picked up the phone and called before her head could make her reconsider. "I'm not a romantic person, Greg. I've never believed there was a perfect match out there for me, but you've embedded yourself in my subconscious. I've been waiting for you."

She packed a small bag that evening and departed King's Cross for Leeds on the 9:05 train the next morning. Her carriage was alive with cheery people, a group of Americans on a walking holiday and two families with young children. Carolyn acknowledged them, then kept to herself, watching the procession of towns and green spaces. She'd never before considered the abundance of life that existed north of London.

As the train slowed at Leeds Station, her heart began to race. She calmed herself. *I've traveled to a place three hours north of London. I'm meeting a respectable man who's going to show me the countryside. I've no obliga-*

31

tions whatsoever. Not a completely accurate characterization of her visit, but the venture seemed less intimidating when she thought of it that way.

Greg, in a long-sleeved polo shirt, his hair ruffled by the wind, stood peering into the throng that swarmed from the station. When Carolyn waved and called his name, a smile lit his face and he walked toward her. "Welcome to Yorkshire." He took her bag. "This is all you've brought? You travel light."

"I'm only staying for two days. I won't need much."

He opened the boot of a little red Sunbeam and deposited the case. "It's not the car I would've expected for you," she said.

"Oh, once in a while, I surprise people."

They drove north from the station—past government and university buildings, terraced houses, blocks of flats, shops. "Leeds is larger than I expected," Carolyn said. "A small city."

"We in Yorkshire consider it a rather large city."

"Yes, of course." Within twenty minutes, they'd left behind every trace of urban life. Greg turned onto a road that curved between green fields edged by dry stone walls and dotted with ewes and lambs. Shadowy hills loomed in the distance. All under a sky so broad it took Carolyn's breath away. "It's beautiful. Grander than the Cotswolds."

"O-Oh, yes."

She watched in awe as Greg effortlessly executed the route's twists and turns. His command of the car might have reassured her, but it didn't. It threw their differences into relief. He was a Northerner who'd lived his whole life in the countryside. She was a London girl who'd rarely ridden in a car, who had seldom in her twenty-three years spent a night away from the city. They'd grown up in two distinct worlds. *I hope I'm not making a mistake.* A sidelong glance at his tender face told her she wasn't. He was a listener, ready to hear whatever she had to say. She chose honesty. "I have a confession to make."

"Go on."

"I'm nervous."

"That's it? That's your confession?"

"Yes. I'm not an adventurous person. I've never done anything like this before."

"Mmm? Never been driven into the wilds of the Dales by a man you hardly knew?"

She looked at her lap. "Now I feel rather foolish."

"Sorry. I was hoping to make you laugh. You needn't feel foolish. Second guessing one's decisions is human, don't you think?"

"Yes, you're right . . . and you'll find I do have a sense of humor hidden somewhere among my second guesses."

They traversed the miles in silence, passing farmsteads and the occasional stand of trees, until they reached Chapman Bridge. "This is my village." Greg pointed out a small stone building on the high Street. "That's the sweet shop where I spent my threepence each Saturday, and the barber in the building opposite cut my hair once a month." He drove along the busy street lined with tidy shops, crossed a river, and headed north into the countryside.

Fifteen minutes later, he turned onto a private path and stopped the car at the front door of an ancient limestone house. "This is yours?" Carolyn asked.

"It is."

"You said a large cottage, but I envisioned something smaller."

"Oh, it's spacious. Could sleep twelve at a pinch."

Inside, creamy yellow walls contrasted with honey-colored wood-work. Carolyn ran her fingers along a deep windowsill and stooped to touch the floor. "The finish is like satin. You've done all this?"

"Yes. I've completed the ground floor. Haven't got to the bedrooms yet." He carried her bag to the stairway. "Follow me. I have renovated the lavatory. It now has a modern shower, and you'll be the first guest to enjoy it."

The small room at the top of the stairs echoed the ground floor's simple style. Pale yellow walls, floor and windowsill of smooth golden wood, a shower lined with white tiles, and a beveled mirror over an unadorned pedestal sink. "It's beautiful," she marveled. "Pristine."

At the end of the hall, Greg opened the door of a room papered in faded pink and green floral. "Quite modest, but the bed faces east. You'll get the morning light." He looked at his watch. "You can arrange your belongings. I'm going downstairs to ring Mum and Dad. They're looking forward to meeting you."

Carolyn returned to the bathroom and set her vanity bag on the windowsill. *His mum and dad are looking forward to meeting me?* She smiled at herself in the mirror, smoothed her hair. *I was with Geoffrey for the better part of a year, and we never seriously considered meeting each other's parents.*

They took a three-minute drive to a small stone cottage where the smiling couple stood at the front door waiting to greet them. "Mum, Dad, this is Carolyn."

Greg's mother, a tiny, bright-faced woman, took a step forward. "I'm Lizzie." She touched the arm of her handsome, weathered husband. "And this is James. Come right in. The scones are almost ready."

In the cheery green and yellow kitchen, a kettle whistled and released a cloud of steam. Lizzie hurried to the oven and pulled out a cast iron tray of fragrant, currant-studded scones while James poured the water into a red teapot. The vibrant colors, the noise, the bustle of activity were in contrast to the serenity of Greg's cottage. *But he plans to raise a family there. It won't always be serene.*

They ate scones with butter and honey while Lizzie talked. "Greg says you've not visited the Dales before. It's a grand place to walk. Do you like walking?"

"I do."

"Then you and Greg are a good match. He's a great walker."

James nodded. "Aye, and a theatre lover. Greg mentioned you the day after the *Hamlet* production, and everything he said from that day on led us to believe you might be the lass for him. The only problem was that young man of yours. He-" Lizzie cleared her throat to cut him off, and Carolyn turned to gauge Greg's reaction. He smiled at her and took a drink of tea.

<hr />

"You talked to them about Geoffrey," Carolyn said as they walked to the car.

Greg shrugged. "Not much. I didn't remember his name, but I did consider him an obstacle, one I ultimately decided to disregard."

"Thank you for that."

He grinned. "Not at all."

Back at his house, he looked her up and down. "I'm not planning a strenuous walk, but I hope you've packed something sturdier than that dress."

"Oh, no. I haven't. Just another dress quite like this one." *What a fool I must seem.* She attempted a smile and pointed at her slingback flats. "And no proper shoes. I don't know what I was thinking."

"Ahh, don't beat yourself up. You've brought a city girl's style and elegance to our part of the world." He patted her shoulder. "Let's have a look round the house for left-behind clothes."

Twenty minutes later Carolyn stood assessing herself in the bedroom mirror. The women's trousers and soft blue shirt Greg found in the kitchen cupboard had hung loose on her, but they were fine once she tucked in the shirt and tightened a belt around her waist. The boots and socks were a passable fit. Though a bit uncertain of her ability to carry out the role she was dressed for, she put on a confident face and walked from the room. Greg, waiting at the foot of the stairs, let out a whistle of admiration. "You've transformed those clothes—given them a new lease of life."

They set out through the hills on the western edge of the property and clambered to the top of a ridge. Carolyn caught her breath. "Quite a change from walking on pavement. I need to work on my stamina— climb Primrose Hill or walk through Hampstead Heath from time to time."

The descent was even more arduous than the climb. "You sit and recover while I make tea," Greg said when they reached the cottage after more than an hour of dodging rocks and brambles. He peeled and cut potatoes into chips, spread them across a tray and slid it into the oven. Sliced apples and tossed them in cinnamon, sugar, and flour. Put the kettle on, then fried two eggs. All with no apparent effort.

While they ate their egg and chips, the spicy fragrance of apple crumble filled the air. Carolyn was enchanted. She'd never known a man to put a meal together the way Greg had done. She couldn't do it herself. "Did your mother teach you to cook like this?"

"Mum and Dad both. Everyone pitches in on a farm."

"I don't cook at all. I can make tea and toast, but not a complete meal."

"Spend more time around here, and you'll acquire the knack."

"I'm not sure about that." She laughed. "But you'll soon discover I compensate for my lack of culinary proficiency with a brilliant talent for washing up."

When they walked upstairs at bedtime, Carolyn entered her room and emerged a minute later carrying her case. "I didn't say anything earlier because I didn't know how I'd feel tonight. I'm certain now. I want to sleep with you." She fixed her eyes on Greg's. "Would you like that?"

"O-oh yes." He brushed his lips across her forehead and whispered, "You smell of hyacinths, always." Then lifted her into a long, slow kiss. When at last it ended and they stood face to face, she stared, wide-eyed and silent. Greg smiled and began unbuttoning her shirt. "I've dreamt of this for almost a year."

After they'd made love and lay breathing their mingled scents, he said, "If we were to count every hour we've spent together, we'd not reach twenty. Too soon to say 'I love you,' don't you think?" Before she could respond, he added, "Let's wait till tomorrow."

Carolyn awoke in the night and walked barefoot over creaking floorboards to an open window. The dusky sky was beginning to lighten. *It's the way Greg described it,* "*The long blue twilight verges on the next day's dawn.*" She ran her hand along the timeworn sill and turned back to face the dim room. Images of the future raced through her mind. *In the morning I will say "I love you." We'll ask one another questions and listen to each other's answers. And we'll be silent together.* Sharing stillness with Greg was the most intimate human interaction she'd ever experienced. She turned and looked at him, watched the easy rise and fall of his chest. *Someday, we'll raise a family here.*

THANKSGIVING STORY

1966

The sun had set, and splats of icy rain were hitting Jane's windshield as she drove along a Tompkins County road searching without success for one called Fallbrook. She had left Syracuse at three o'clock with plans to reach Mark Campbell's farm before dark. Obviously, that wouldn't be happening. It seemed that half the side roads were unmarked. She couldn't tell if she'd missed her turn or hadn't yet reached it. She peered hopefully as she approached each corner and, eventually, out of frustration, turned onto one of the unidentified roads. An adventurous person with an excellent sense of direction, Jane was confounded, totally demoralized. She parked her Volvo sedan and burst into tears. *Mark is at home with his family waiting for me, his supposedly competent, self-assured girlfriend, while I sit crying in my car.* She looked around. The closest house sat atop a nearby hill. Ablaze with lights, it was certainly connected to a road, but there was no driveway in sight. *There has to be one somewhere*, she thought. She decided to explore on foot. *If I don't find a path within a few minutes, I'll come back and recalibrate.*

She moved her car well off the road and grabbed her overnight bag, then had a second thought and stowed it in the trunk with the three bottles of wine that were to be her contribution to the next day's feast. She locked up and set out, pondering the events that had led her to this dark country road.

Mark had been Jane's plant biochemistry professor during spring term of her junior year. He was so young looking that she wondered how he could possibly have earned a PhD. Earnest and charismatic, he somehow managed to hold the whole class spellbound as he discussed the molecular function of plants. Occasionally, at the end of a lecture, he'd mention his Finger Lakes farm, and it was his passion for growing asparagus and peas and strawberries that impressed Jane. One morning after class, she made a comment about his being the kind of man she wanted to marry, and he embarrassed her with his response. "Well, we'll have to wait until you graduate for that. I can't date a student, let alone marry one." She laughed and so did he, and the incident seemed forgotten until the following year.

He called her in June. "I don't think either of us is ready to think about marriage, but since you're no longer a student, maybe we could see each other from time to time." Before she had a chance to reply, he added, "We could meet at the Chapter House for a drink tonight if you're free."

They hit it off in a casual, friendly way. Got together several times throughout the summer, each meeting lighthearted and uneventful.

When Jane announced she'd been offered a job teaching biology in Syracuse and would be moving at the end of August, Mark invited her to visit his farm before she left Ithaca.

He picked her up on Friday afternoon, the week before her move. Twenty-five minutes from town, they pulled to a stop on a gravel path bordered by woods on one side and cultivated fields on the other. A path that curved through the largest pumpkin patch Jane had ever seen led to a grassy lawn and a white clapboard house. Mark gave a wave of introduction. "Here it is, Campbell Farm." Her heart thumped with delight as she looked at the big old house—down-at-heel but gracious—surrounded by cultivated fields and a wild looking stretch of woodland. The polar opposite of the subdivision she'd grown up in, where each rectangular lot boasted a story-and-a-half Cape Cod house with a small beech tree in the front yard and two slender maples in the back. A yard with trees large enough to climb had been the unfulfilled dream of her otherwise happy childhood. She looked at Mark in amazement. "You've had all this for your whole life?"

"From age thirteen on."

She laughed out loud. "It's wonderful."

Inside, Mark put *Revolver* on the stereo and started cooking. "I think it's the Beatles' best album yet. And that's saying something." Jane almost confessed she didn't know anything about the content of the Beatles' albums but decided to go with a nod. They ate on the front porch—pasta shaped like little ears tossed with juicy home grown tomatoes, parmesan cheese grated by hand, and slender ribbons of a bright green herb. "It's basil," he told her, "a staple in Italian cooking." After dinner, he made espresso in a noisy little aluminum pot he called a moka. Everything about the visit delighted her.

Back at her apartment, Jane curled up with *Silent Spring*, a book she'd started rereading earlier that day, but she couldn't stay focused on the state of the planet. She kept pausing to assess the state of her emotions. She'd never met anyone quite like Mark. *I wish we could start over, readjust our relationship.* She wrote him a note: Mark, I had a wonderful time with you today. Thank you for the tour of the farm and the delicious dinner. Who knew? On top of all your other skills, you're a gourmet cook. I've enjoyed our last couple of months. I hope we can stay in touch. Jane.

She read it over before putting it in an envelope. *It's okay*, she thought. *Friendly, but not too pushy. No silly comments about marriage for him to make a joke about.*

His response arrived on Thursday: Jane, last year I observed you three days a week for a term. You set an enthusiastic tone for the entire class— led by example. I always looked forward to your intelligent comments, but it wasn't until the day you said I was the kind of man you wanted to marry that I admitted to myself I was attracted to you. It took me aback, so I attempted what I hoped you'd consider a humorous reply. For some reason, when I finally called you, I started our relationship in a just friends mode and never shook free of it. When we said good-bye on Friday night, I was struck by a bolt of truth. I would like more than friendship. Consider this my opening salvo. I look forward to your response. Best, Mark.

She wrote him the next day: Mark, that day after class I didn't plan to say you were exactly the kind of man I'd like to marry. The words burst right out of me, but I wasn't joking. I knew that if and when I married, I'd want someone connected to the earth like you are. Something more than friendship sounds good to me. Let's give it a try. Call me. Jane.

He called her, and she called him. They talked about the past as they worked on their present. Mark's farm was the center of his life. He'd discovered himself as he expanded it from a small garden he planted at age thirteen to over twenty productive acres. Jane was a sister to four rambunctious older brothers who'd teased, inspired, and championed her. She concentrated on winning arm wrestling contests and foot races as a child, on excelling academically as a teenager. Physical vigor and mental fortitude were what she strived for.

In his third phone call, Mark opened up. "I have a way of scanning my students' faces, connecting to one and then another as I talk. But whenever I reached your elegant face, your beautiful brown eyes, I couldn't move on. I'd have to look down at my notes—something unheard of for me—in order to continue my lecture. I was so focused on maintaining my professorial stance that I ignored what should have been a clue to my feelings."

In less than a minute, he'd both complimented her and revealed himself. Jane was so bewildered she couldn't find words to reciprocate. Just stammered a sort of thank you and said goodbye. She went into the bathroom and looked in the mirror, tucked her hair behind her ears, then shook it loose. Tipped her head from side to side. *He's wrong. I can't detect a jot of elegance.* Then laughed. *But my eyes really are quite nice.*

For the next two months, they talked most days, saw each other once a week. But on the second weekend in November Jane bowed out of a string quartet performance they'd been looking forward to. "I'm buried in work. I'll end up behind all week if I take Saturday off."

The following Friday, Mark cancelled a dinner. "We'll make up for lost time next week," he said. "I'll cook Thanksgiving dinner for my parents and my sister, Maeve. You can be my sous-chef."

That's how Jane came to be walking on the soft shoulder of a country road searching for a path through the fields that might lead up to the warm, bright house and a phone. She looked down at the Italian loafers she'd put on three hours earlier. So much for impressing Mark's family with her sense of style. *When—if—I meet them, I'll be sopping wet, and these shoes'll be caked with mud.* Her earlier tearful outburst had been triggered by embarrassment. She wasn't the kind of person who got lost and showed up late for engagements. Now uneasiness, verging on fear, displaced her vanity. She envisioned a patrolman pulling up beside her and saying, *"Miss, what are you doing walking along a country road on a night like this?"* She would manage to refrain from hugging the officer and ask him to make a phone call for her. Within minutes, Mark would show up and lead her to his house. It was a fantasy. There wasn't a car in sight.

God, I want a flashlight, an umbrella, a cup of steaming coffee. And then she saw it, a gravel path that led away from the muddy shoulder. She looked up at the beckoning house and tried to guess how long it might take to reach it. Jane was five foot nine with a long stride and walked four miles an hour with ease, but given the darkness and steep incline, she knew she couldn't maintain that pace. So maybe half an hour—thirty cold, wet minutes—before she could call Mark and have the homeowner explain the location to him. By the time he and she got back to her car and arrived at his place, it would be eight o'clock. *If I'm lucky. If this path actually leads to the house.*

She took a deep breath and began her upward trudge. Encouraged, she laughed at her predicament, then thought of Mark. He wasn't a worrier, but what must he be thinking? *Well, I'm not a worrier either. Tomorrow this will be nothing more than a funny story, a Thanksgiving story.* She abandoned all caution, focused on the goal ahead rather than the path beneath her feet, and promptly stepped into a rut. She caught herself with one hand and marched on looking straight ahead. *Why look down? I couldn't see my feet if I tried.* Cold and hungry, but confident, she kept her eyes on the beacon at the top of the hill. Imagined the scene inside the house, parents and children laughing as they sat down to dinner. *They'll invite me in, take my wet jacket, offer me something hot to drink, and I'll call Mark.* While they all waited for him to show up, she'd recount her long wet trek up the hill.

Hurrying up the slope, she slipped on the wet gravel. Maintained her balance, but it was a wake-up call. *Relax, Jane, you're almost there.* She slowed down to a steady walk. The rain had stopped, the clouds dispersed, and an almost full moon revealed the world around her. Shone down on a thicket of brambles and leafless trees to the left of the path and lit up an empty field prepared for winter on the right. It was really quite beautiful. Under other circumstances, the walk would be a pleasure. *Actually, I'm enjoying it right now.*

She looked across the cold, bare tract and wondered what might have grown there in the summer. She envisioned it on a humid August day, the field alive with huge green leaves on exuberant vines and hundreds of pumpkins waiting for harvest. *I know this place. I know this place.* She could make out a sign at the end of the lane but couldn't read it. *I don't have to. I know what it says, Campbell Farm.* The man waiting patiently inside the brightly lit house beyond the sign wasn't the kind of man she wanted to marry. He was the one. *It's 1966; I'm a modern woman. I'll ask him tonight.* She broke into a run and her voice rang through the frigid air. "Mark, Mark, I'm here."

FOLLOW YOUR HEART

1978

Will Bonham turned seven the first week of summer holidays, and his parents gave him permission to wander the surrounding Yorkshire countryside on his own. They made only two demands—the same ones they'd made of his sister, Sophie, when she was his age—that he behave himself and arrive home each day in time for evening tea.

His destination most afternoons was the neighboring farm—his granddad's. He'd climb up through the bracken to the top of the ridge at the west edge of his parents' property, scramble down the rock-studded hill toward the lush sheep pasture on the southwest corner of the farm, and reach the back yard of the old stone cottage before two o'clock.

It was July, months past lambing season. Shearing had taken place at the beginning of June, and the ewes and their lambs were grazing in the pasture. Granddad spent the long North Yorkshire days mending walls and fences and building a new stone shelter for the sheep. Will was thrilled to fetch and carry for him.

Each day, in the heat of the afternoon, Granddad would wipe his brow with a big blue and white handkerchief and pull out his watch. "Almost half three. Time for tea."

They'd head for the kitchen, a bright room that smelled of oiled boots. On Sundays it smelled of the Lysol Granddad used to clean the floor, but by Mondays it was back to the boot smell that Will loved. He loved most everything about the house. The rippled windowpanes that made the green pastures look wavy and the uneven floorboards that creaked when you walked. The soft, worn upholstery of the rocking chair that faced the hearth. The pantry, with jars of rosy stewed rhubarb and pale yellow pear halves lining its high shelf and a crock of butter, a jar of honey, and a fragrant loaf of whole meal bread on its low one. "You help yourself to bread and honey, son," Granddad would say after the two of them washed their hands. The plates were on open shelves above the painted sideboard, and Will would drag a three-legged wooden stool across the room to reach them.

"How about you, Granddad? Would you like bread and honey, too?"

The answer was always the same. "Yes, indeed, and I'll brew the tea."

Will would cut two thick slices and spread them with butter and honey while the kettle came to a boil. Then they'd wait four minutes and have tea at the scrubbed kitchen table. Men together.

Once in a while, Granddad pointed out reminders of Gran. "This was Lizzie's favorite plant," he'd say of the hoya on the kitchen sill. "Just you wait. Each March it fairly bursts into flower." He'd show off the book-lined shelf in the little alcove he called the library. "Lizzie was a reader. This was her doing."

But aside from those mementos and one photo of Gran in the bedroom, the cottage seemed a man's house to Will. *Nothing fancy here. No cut flowers in vases, no bowls of potpourri on side tables.*

"Do you miss Gran?" he asked one day. "Are you sad that she died?"

"Oh, I miss her. I think of her each morning when I rise, but I'm not sad. Too busy to be sad. I'm as happy as a man can be."

Granddad had started farming sheep at age thirteen. During teatime on those summer afternoons, he told Will of his life. Took him on a journey through the seasons of a shepherd's year. Little by little, he related chapters of the story. Of mending walls and cutting hay while the sheep fattened themselves during the long summer days. Checking the condition of the rams and putting them out for breeding with his ewes in the autumn. Keeping careful watch on the condition of the pregnant ewes throughout the winter. Then lambing, the busiest time of year. Granddad chuckled. "Sheep don't stop lambing when the sun sets. They need watching day and night." Shearing time came in June. Then time to wean the lambs. Let them feed on grass until autumn when they'd be heavy enough to sell. The old man offered the boy a piece of advice. "Of course, a good shepherd must always hold back a few of his most promising young ewes to breed lambs of their own."

Learning the sequence of events that marked a farmer's life opened Will's mind. All the ewes and rams and little lambs he'd seen since his own babyhood were part of a great cycle. He didn't fully understand it, but he longed to be part of the shepherd's world. Lambing season captured his imagination. "Do you think I might help with it next spring?"

"Oh, son, you're a wee lad. Your mum and dad wouldn't allow it. You've got your studies to attend to. And the truth of it is, you're too small to be of help. You'd be in the way." He paused and looked into

Will's eyes. "But you could watch a time or two, at the weekends. That would be fine. What do you think?"

"Yes, it would be fine."

"That's what we'll do."

The last weekend in March of the following spring, Granddad and his collie, Sam, herded the ewes in from the far reaches of the pasture. Organized them in their outdoor paddocks. True to his word, he collected Will on the afternoon of the first Friday in April. The boy stood in the kitchen and pulled a wool cap down over his ears. "I'm all ready for lambing."

"Almost, son. Let's find you an old wax coat to protect that fancy red puffer jacket." He rummaged through the tall kitchen cupboard and pulled out a smallish one. "Here you go," he said. "It was your gran's." He rolled the sleeves and stepped back to regard Will. "Right. Now you're a proper shepherd." They walked outside and began their trek. Early on, they came upon a ewe who'd lambed on her own; Granddad patted her as the lamb stood suckling, its tail flapping. "Well done," he said and walked on.

"Should we stay and watch a while to be sure everything's all right?" Will asked.

"No, we needn't. We'll stop by for a look later, but not to worry. Dalesbreds are excellent mothers. The shepherd's role is to help those in difficulty." They continued walking, stopping occasionally to examine a ewe. "Not quite ready," the old man would say. When they'd looked them all over, he said, "Well, that's enough for now. Good time for tea and a bit of rest. Save our energy for later."

Tea was to be a hearty one. Granddad peeled three potatoes and cut them into slices, then scattered them on a greased cast iron tray that he slid into the hot oven. After a quarter hour, he threw two handfuls of chopped onions over the chips. Half an hour later he pulled out the baking tray and formed two gaps in the golden brown masterpiece. "Son, you know how to crack an egg, right?" The boy nodded. "Then get us a couple of large ones and go to it." Granddad popped the sheet into the oven for another five minutes to cook the eggs. It was Will's best tea ever.

Back outside, they carried on walking and watching. Twice they discovered a ewe tending a new lamb. It all went like clockwork until they heard a ewe bleating in distress as she paced. Granddad patted her. "Having a hard time, are you?" He spoke softly and began to stroke her. Reached in under her tail and gave a pull. Then another. After each pull he let the ewe lick his bloody hands and spoke in a low voice, "Good girl." Patiently, over and over, he repeated the actions. Will watched the slow process, taking anxious breaths, until at last Granddad pulled out the wet lamb and laid it by the ewe's head. He patted the lamb and then the ewe. Tired as she was, she began to lick. "Aye, there's a good girl." The old man glowed with satisfaction. "She's lambed a big healthy boy."

Will gazed, awestruck. *Someday I'll do that.* They continued walking through the cold April night until the boy could scarcely stand. Granddad carried him into the house, and they both slept a few hours before starting the watch all over again.

———◆———

Eventually, Will did lamb a sheep, dozens of them, but that experience was years in coming. In the meantime, he learned and carried out the varied chores of a sheep farmer. At his first shearing, he grabbed the fleeces as Granddad tossed them aside. Rolled them and stuffed them into a burlap bag. "How many pounds do we make per fleece?" he asked after bagging almost two hundred of them.

"Fifty pence if we're lucky. But owt's better than nowt. It's why I shear 'em myself. Save paying an outsider. And part of the profit is your doing, Will. Weren't for you, I'd be paying some other lad to help out."

Will heeded the rhythm of the shepherd's year after school and during holidays. He offered an extra pair of hands on the cool days and cold nights of April lambing. Bonded with the collie, who taught him to herd the flock. Each June, he dragged sheep to the board for a daylong shearing marathon. A week later he'd help treat the newly sheared sheep for maggots. He cut and baled sweet-smelling hay under the midsummer sun and carried the bales over frosty fields for winter feeding.

"When Dad was a boy, did he ever help with the farming like I do?" he asked one day.

"Oh yes, Greg was a great help when he was a lad."

"Why did he give it up? Why is he a teacher?"

"He took heed of his heart, Will, as we each must do."

At last, on a cold still night when he was eleven, Will had his turn. A ewe lay on her side. The lamb's head and one leg were emerging. "Help her, son. You can do it. Take hold of that leg with your left hand and go for the other one with your right." With a pounding heart, Will reached in and Granddad talked him through it. "Fetch that turned-back front leg."

Will summoned every scrap of concentration he possessed. "I have it."

"Right. There you go. Now flip it forward and pull." Will took a shaky breath and slowly pulled on the two legs with the head between them. Granddad patted his shoulder. "Well done, son. Give her a break, then pull again." One more long, slow pull and the lamb slipped out. Will beamed and plopped it in front of the ewe, who set to licking furiously.

He looked down at the lamb he'd helped bring into the world and up at the inky sky hung with a thousand stars. Breathed in the frigid air of the North Yorkshire night. Overcome by the richness of life, he made up his mind. *I'm going to be a shepherd when I'm grown. I'll tell Dad tomorrow morning.*

As it turned out, he didn't make his announcement at breakfast. Worried that his father might feel criticized for the way he'd chosen to live his own life, Will confessed the plan to his mother after his dad left for work. He seethed with emotion. "I don't want to live the way he does. Leaving two first-class herding dogs with nothing to do but sleep while he teaches school. He wastes those dogs, Mum. I'd never do that." His voice went soft. "I want to farm sheep. Do you think Dad will feel bad when I tell him?"

"No, dear. Say you want to be a shepherd when you're grown. Dad will understand. He'll be proud of you." She brushed a dark curl back from Will's forehead. "You needn't mention the part about his wasting the collies."

She was right. When his dad heard the plan, he smiled. "That sounds fine, son. Mustn't neglect your studies though. Your grandfather will agree with me on that."

Granddad did agree. One afternoon he went to his little library shelf and pulled out a black volume with gold lettering on the spine. *The Complete Shakespeare,* like the one Will's dad read from. "It was your gran's," he said. "She read me sonnets from it. Started reading *Macbeth* aloud, but she didn't live to finish." He opened the heavy book across the palm of his strong right hand and, with his left thumb, flipped to a page marked with a brown oak leaf. "Happen you could take up reading where she left off. It's a powerful story."

"It is. Dad read it to Sophie and me. I can't read as well as he does, but I'll give it a go."

"Right. No one can say I'm neglecting your book learning."

Will thrived academically. So much so, that when his parents informed the school of his dedication to farming and requested he be given time off when lambing season came round each spring, the head teacher praised the boy's initiative. "Of course, he should be free to explore that facet of life."

<hr />

The autumn he was sixteen and began revision for his A levels, Granddad needed more help than Will had time to offer. Jake, a teenaged neighbor, pitched in, and the three of them managed the work together. Will loved every hour he spent on the farm, but he was developing a passion for what Granddad called *book learning* as well. The words of Shakespeare and Yeats thrilled him. A new aspiration arose. "Do you think I could go to university and come back after and run the farm?"

"Anything's possible," Granddad replied.

He was in the midst of researching his plans for the future—how he might study at Oxford and come home to work on holidays—when his grandfather died of myocardial infarction. Along with the crushing pain of loss came facts of life Will wasn't ready for. He and Jake would continue working, but lambing season was around the corner—the farm needed a full time manager. His dad found a buyer.

"It's disloyal, isn't it? Letting the farm go to a stranger. I should take charge."

"Son, there's no way a sixteen-year-old in the sixth form could run the farm. And we're not letting it go to a stranger. Martin, the buyer, knew

Granddad for years. He loves the earth and sheep the way you do. You'll be free to work with him whenever you have time."

"What if the dream of farming slips away from me? What if I'm not resolute enough to hold on to it?"

"A month ago you were talking to Granddad about Oxford. He was proud that his grandson was applying to such a great university. Do you still want that?"

"Yes, I do."

"Then go for it and give it your best. You'll hold fast to the dream if it's right for you. Whatever you decide, you've had a remarkable run. You've followed your heart, and you must carry on doing that. It's what Granddad would want for you."

On a visit to the farm, years after graduating from Oxford, Will climbed through the bracken to the top of the ridge with his pregnant wife and surveyed the lush meadows that bordered his granddad's stone cottage. "You miss him," she said. "You're feeling sad, aren't you?" She turned to look down the hill, and Will stood behind her, his hands cradling her belly.

"I do miss Granddad. I think of him—what he shared with me—every day, but I'm not sad. I'm as happy as a man can be."

BEST FRIENDS,
INTERRUPTED

1992

Last Friday was graduation day at Cremona Senior High School. We had the traditional ceremony where we filed across the stage and got our diplomas and all the awards and scholarships were announced. No one was surprised by who was named valedictorian and won a full-ride scholarship to Hunter College in New York City. The student who walked away with those honors was my best friend, Ellie. *Was*, as in *used to be.*

She and I met the first day of kindergarten while we waited on the playground for the school bell to ring. She had blonde braids with all these curls poking out and waving around her face. Her red tights were baggy at the knees and ankles, and she was wearing navy blue Keds, which weren't nearly as cool as my Nikes. But she looked happier than any other kid on the playground so I decided to talk to her. "My name is Amy. What's yours?"

Her face opened into the widest smile I'd ever seen. "Ellie O'Neal. I'm starting kindergarten today." She held up a book. "I brought *The Giving Tree*."

"For show and tell?"

She looked confused for a second, then shook her head emphatically. "No, for reading class. I'm just learning. The teacher will help me."

I felt a little sorry for her. Her braids were messy, her tights were loose, her shoes were old-fashioned, and she thought that kindergarten teachers taught their students to read real books like *The Giving Tree*. I guessed she didn't have a big brother or sister to help her pick out clothes or fill her in on what kindergarten was like. I could've told her, but I didn't want to be a know-it-all. I thought, *She'll find out soon enough*.

After two days, she quit carrying the book with her. "My mom's teaching me to read the hard words at night after dinner," she told me one afternoon as she connected dots to make a giant maple leaf on one of those boring kindergarten worksheets.

Ellie complied with school guidelines, but never—from kindergarten to the beginning of twelfth grade—did she conform in any way. She marched to her own drum, followed her own agenda. Wore deliberately mismatched socks at age seven and mid-thigh length tee shirts she'd painted herself at twelve. She had strong opinions and she voiced them. Convinced our ninth grade English teacher to change our Shakespeare assignment from *Julius Caesar*, a play he didn't seem to like, to

The Tempest, which he loved. She never once used a blow dryer to tame her curls. And she was always the happiest kid in our class.

———◆———

When we met, Ellie knew next to nothing about life in the twentieth century. The day after visiting my house for the first time, she said, "I asked my mom about television."

"What did you ask her?"

"Why some people have one. Why we don't. If she thinks TVs are bad."

"And what'd she say?"

"That there are all kinds of people. That good people can like different things. She and Dad think we have enough to entertain us without a TV."

"In other words, you're not going to get one."

She shrugged. "I guess not. But she said it's okay if I watch yours." She hardly ever did though. I guess she had enough to entertain her without it.

Ellie and her brother had a lot of stuff—more books than anyone I knew, a record player and hundreds of records, a piano their dad played while they all sang, and an extra long dock stretching out over the lake—but nothing modern. They didn't have a microwave or a CD player. They didn't use plastic wrap. Didn't shop in malls or eat in restaurants. Ellie'd never been to Disney World or New York City or even Syracuse.

We were eight years old, sitting on her bed taking turns reading *Stuart Little* aloud, when she told me she didn't mind at all that she'd never gone on a vacation. "I like it here in the Finger Lakes," she said. "Besides, we don't have enough money for trips because we have two mortgages."

I'd never heard that word before. "What's a mortgage?"

"The money a grown-up owes the bank for a house."

The next day I asked my mom if she and Dad had one. She gave me a funny look. "Of course."

"I think you should've told me."

"Who talks to their third grader about mortgages?"

"The O'Neals do."

"Oh, Amy, they're a special sort of parents." Over the years, she and my dad chatted with Ellie's mom and dad when they dropped us off or picked us up. Our families trusted each other with their kids but never bonded. They never spent a weekend afternoon together, never shared a meal. It was okay with me. I liked having Ellie and her family to myself.

<hr />

From age five to seventeen, I spent almost as much time in her family's white clapboard house and their one-room lakefront cottage as I did with my own family. I swam in the lake, worked in the garden, and learned the words to all the old 1960s rock songs with the O'Neals. Ellie and I read to each other. The two of us worked our way through the children's section of the library, from *Charlotte's Web* to *The Chronicles of Narnia,* and at age thirteen we started a haphazard exploration of the adult collection.

In ninth grade, I fueled my adolescent fantasies with a subscription to *Seventeen.* I knew it wouldn't be to Ellie's taste, but I showed her the April issue—we always shared whatever we were reading. She politely perused the magazine page by page until she reached "Dealing with Swimsuit Anxiety." At that point, she couldn't contain herself. She threw her head back and laughed. "Anyone with swimsuit anxiety probably has other issues to deal with first." She was right. Ellie was cool—without even trying to be.

That year I started going to parties on Saturday nights. I always invited Ellie. "Come with me. You'll have fun."

"Nah, you go on. You can tell me about it tomorrow." The next day she'd listen with rapt attention while I recreated the whole evening for her. She'd say, "Yeah, it does sound like fun." And she meant it. Ellie never told a lie. But she never went to one of those parties. She'd flash her wide, open smile and shrug. "I'm not a party kind of girl."

The two of us read together at least once a week until the end of our sophomore year. That summer, Ellie fell in love with Ethan, a preppy guy who shared her devotion to literature. She started reading with him, and I hardly saw her for three months. Then at the end of August, he left and went back to his fancy school—I knew all along that's what he'd do. She seemed heartbroken for a while, but within a month her smile returned. She was happy again, and she'd changed. In a good way. I'd always dreamed about growing up and leaving home, but the future hadn't been anywhere on Ellie's radar. It had taken her almost forever, but she was finally excited about the wonders that lay ahead. We were even better friends than before—planning our escape from small-town monotony—imagining our brilliant lives.

Last fall, we started our senior year flying high. We were making exciting decisions about life beyond high school. We decided we'd each go our own way and explore new worlds, but we'd always be best friends.

Then one terrible afternoon, everything changed. On the first Saturday in October, Ellie's dad and brother died in a fire. Half of her wonderful family was gone—and all of her joy. She stayed out of school for a week. The day she came back, I waited by her locker. I was nervous. I'd thought hard about what I'd say. I couldn't say I knew how bad she felt. Because I didn't. Or how great her dad and brother were. That would've made her hurt all the more. I wasn't going to say time would make her feel better. That sounded phony, and she wouldn't have believed it. I decided to say, "I love you, Ellie." Because it was true. But I didn't get to tell her. When she saw me waiting, she averted her eyes and walked on by. I tried again and then again. I finally gave up.

She receded from life. Quit leading discussions and asking awesome questions in class. She didn't say a word, just turned in her assignments and disappeared when the school bell rang at the end of the day.

When we all marched into the auditorium for graduation yesterday, our parents stood up and turned to watch the procession. Ellie's mom reached out and squeezed my hand as I passed. The look on her face—happy and proud and sad all at once—almost made me cry, but I held the tears back. And I did it again while the senior choir sang "Forever Young." It wasn't until Ellie accepted her awards that I actually cried. She smiled, but it wasn't the joyful smile she'd flashed her whole life. I thought, *She's not Ellie any more. She's some other girl,* and tears slipped down my cheeks.

My mom thinks I should try to contact her again now that school's out. Call, or maybe walk over to her house and knock on the door. I can't. Ellie's smile lit up the world. She was the happiest girl I ever knew. This other girl is the saddest. Ellie had dreams. This girl's not the one who dreamed them. Ellie had a father and a brother who loved her. This girl doesn't. My saying "I love you" wouldn't have made things right for Ellie last October, and neither will saying it now. So I won't. I can't.

Mom says that my memories of happy days with Ellie will never disappear, and that even though Ellie can't think about them now, her memories will last, too. That one day when she's walking down a street somewhere, she'll remember something we did together, and she'll laugh out loud. "Whether you believe it or not, you and Ellie will always be connected. The friendship you've shared will bless you both forever."

It sounds like one of those sweet things adults say, but my mom's not the mushy type at all. She's actually pretty smart. Maybe she's right. I can't change anything now, but maybe this is only an interruption. Maybe Ellie and I will be friends again someday. Mom's words make me feel better. I think that's called hope.

WE'RE GOING
TO BE FINE

1986

R uth Thielen, the sixth-grade Gifted and Talented teacher at PS
168 in the Bronx, had arranged a presentation for her class on the
third Tuesday in May. Mira, an energetic graduate student from Ford-
ham, was introducing *Twelfth Night*, the play the students would read in
preparation for seeing a production at the Delacorte Theatre. Her athletic
depiction of mistaken identity and romantic confusion, augmented by
props and costume changes, captivated the kids. Each time she called for
a volunteer, they vied with one another for a chance to perform. Ruth
was thrilled. *It's perfect.*

In the midst of the happy mayhem, she noticed that Laura Weber,
her most consistently enthusiastic student, wasn't participating. It had

been Laura, always up for a challenge, who'd suggested the class study a work they could later watch at Shakespeare in the Park. *I'd expect her to be in the thick of the action. I hope she didn't get bad news at the principal's office.*

The school secretary had summoned Laura at one forty-five. "I'll be back in time for the presentation," she'd said with a thumbs-up as she hurried from the classroom. When she returned ten minutes later looking subdued, Ruth paid it no mind. Even a well-balanced twelve-year-old could be all over the map emotionally.

But something was definitely amiss. As the other students cheered a slapstick sword fight, Laura, seemingly unaware of the clamor, sat at her desk holding a note. She read it, then carefully folded it into a square and tucked it into her shirt pocket. For the next half hour, her gaze alternated between the classroom door and the clock on the wall.

I'll try to talk to her before she leaves today, Ruth thought. *She's a straightforward child. Maybe she'll share what's on her mind.*

Laura didn't want to talk. She exited in a hurry amidst a group of boisterous classmates and ran most of the eight blocks to her house. Only slowed down when she could see her mother sitting on the stoop. She needed to catch her breath, to save her energy for talking. She walked the last half block. "Mom," she called as she got close. Carla Weber, a statuesque brunette, stood up and held out her arms. Laura buried her face in her mother's soft breasts. "Oh, Mom. Oh, Mom," she cried.

Carla wiped Laura's face with a tissue and took her hand. "Let's talk."

"Can we go inside?" Laura asked.

"Yes, for just a little while so we can say goodbye, like I wrote in the note. Aunt Doreen helped me move my things out this afternoon. Dad doesn't want me in the house."

"You mean you can't even visit? I won't see you anymore?" The tears that had subsided began to flow again.

"Not here at the house. But we'll still see each other. We can meet at Doreen's place or at the cafe for a soda."

"Why? Why is Dad doing this?"

They walked inside and sat on the sofa. Carla pulled her daughter close. "It's my fault. I've been seeing Manny again. I told Dad this morning after you left for school."

"Mom," Laura's voice rose in alarm. "Why? That was all over last year. Dad forgave you and everything."

"He did. Your dad's a big-hearted man, but this time it's too much for him to bear."

"Tell him you'll stop. Promise him."

"I did, but that's what I said the last time. Then I broke my promise. Dad doesn't trust me anymore."

"But do you still love him?"

"I do."

"So why do you keep seeing Manny?"

"I don't know how to explain it to you." Carla sighed. "It's complicated."

Laura bit her lip. "Is it about sex?"

"That's part of it."

"Then stop the sex part," she pleaded. "Can't you just be Manny's friend?"

"No," Carla said. "That's not how it works."

Laura turned away and traced a rose on the chintz covered sofa pillow. "Where will you live?" she asked.

"I'm sleeping on Doreen's Murphy bed tonight. Then I'm going to stay with Manny for a while."

"No-o, you can't." Her voice rose again. "He lives all the way down in Brooklyn." She laid her face in her mother's lap and sobbed. "My heart is broken, Mom. And Dad's will be too. And yours. Our life is ruined."

Carla wiped away her own tears and took Laura's face in her hands. "I love you. Your father loves you. Our life is going to be different, but it's not ruined. We'll be fine." She stood up. "I have to leave now. I don't want to face Aunt Elaine again, so I'd like you to carry up the little stepladder I borrowed from her and Aunt Susie. Can you do that favor for me?"

"Yeah. Will I see you tomorrow?"

"No, but soon. You take care of Daddy tonight, okay?"

"I will. But I'm going to miss you. And even if he doesn't know it yet, Dad will too. We both will."

"I know." Carla kissed Laura's forehead and walked to the door. "And I'll miss you. I love you."

"I love you too, Mom." She reached out for her mother's hand. "Bye."

"Bye, sweetie . . . bye." She let go of Laura's hand, turned, and walked out the door.

Laura whispered, "Mom doesn't live here any more."

———————◆———————

Carla reached the corner and turned back to look at the house where she'd lived for thirteen years. Maybe wave to Laura. But the stoop was empty. Her daughter was inside, alone. *Probably better this way. What good would one last wave do either of us?* She pulled a tissue from her purse and blew her nose. *What did I expect Stan to do when I said I'd been with Manny twice in the past month?* She couldn't erase the image of sadness dropping over his face as she told him. *Did I actually think he'd believe me when I said it wouldn't happen again?* She scoffed. *I hardly believed it myself. And giving Laura the news in a note she'd read at school. What's wrong with me?* She thought about her daughter, coping with a situation no twelve-year-old should have to deal with—that she couldn't possibly understand—and her tears welled up. *My god, I can't understand it myself.* She wiped her eyes and kept walking.

Doreen Rinaldi had blocked out three hours to help Carla move house, but it didn't take that long. So there she was, back at the shop, with almost two hours before her next haircut. Tina, the young woman she'd hired to answer the phone and tidy up, stopped sweeping. "Wow, that was fast."

"Yeah," Doreen said as she poured herself a cup of coffee, "Carla didn't take anything but her clothes and a couple boxes of mementos. Left everything else for Stan and Laura. She feels so guilty about sleeping with Manny."

"Well, she should. Her kid—totally innocent—is the one who'll suffer most. She's the one I feel for."

"Yeah, me too. Laura's always been a feisty girl, but this is gonna be real hard on her. My dad used to say, 'What doesn't kill you, makes you stronger.' I hope it's true. I hope Laura ends up stronger."

Doreen carried her coffee out to the bistro table in front of the salon. Lit a cigarette and thought about Carla, her best friend for almost thirty years. About the old days. Of herself as a girl, the spunky one—rough around the edges—but full of common sense. Carla had been the sweet one, always with a smile. And she was gifted. With a few strokes of a pencil or a stick of charcoal, she could create a person's face or an entire scene on a sheet of paper. But she was hard on herself. Never believed she was as good as she should be. *This isn't gonna be easy for her, either.*

Laura walked into her parents' bedroom and stared into the half-empty closet. Opened a dresser drawer and breathed in the scent of her mother. Then closed it with a quick shove. *I don't want Mom's smell to go away.* She rinsed her face in the kitchen sink and looked at the stepladder propped against the wall near the front door. She dreaded returning it, but she had to. If she didn't, Aunt Elaine would blame her mom. She walked slowly up the stairs. *Aunt Susie is nice, but Elaine always talks bad about Mom. After what happened today, she'll talk even worse than usual. Maybe Susie will answer,* she thought as she rang the bell. But Elaine opened the door.

"Here's your stepladder."

Her aunt took it without a thank you. "So, I guess your mom's all moved out. You two weren't exciting enough for the likes of her." She clicked her tongue in disapproval. "Well, Stanley won't have to put up with her lies anymore."

"She didn't lie. She told Dad the truth. That's why she had to leave."

"Hmph. Where's she staying?"

"At Aunt Doreen's." Elaine and Susie didn't need to know the part about Manny's place.

"Aunt Doreen," Elaine sneered. "She's not your aunt."

Laura's dark eyes flashed. "She's Mom's best friend. Ever since first grade. I can call her *aunt* if I want to."

"Laura, you're coming very close to sassing. You need to learn to mind your mouth."

Susie walked in from the kitchen, drying her hands on a dishtowel. "Elaine, you need to learn to mind your manners. You could invite the child in." She put her arm around Laura and smoothed her hair. "I'm so sorry you have to go through this."

"It's okay. Dad and Mom and I all love each other. We're going to be fine." She held back her tears until she got downstairs. In the privacy of her room, she threw herself on the bed and sobbed.

◆

On Thursday afternoon, Laura stopped at Doreen's salon. "Mom hasn't called or left me a note at school or anything. I'm worried. Is she okay? Did she move to Brooklyn?"

"Yeah, she did. She found a job at a salon there and started work this morning. She's got a lot on her plate right now. She'll call you as soon as she has time."

"Does she remember my recital is on Sunday? At one thirty at the Jewish center? I hope she doesn't have to work that day."

"Yes, she knows. She and I'll come together. Would you like a soda?"

"No, not now. I'm going up to Aunt Susie and Elaine's to practice on their piano before Dad gets home. He's getting off early today." She forced a little smile. "We're going for pizza."

◆

For two days, Laura had avoided meaningful conversation with her dad. *I'm pretty good at it*, she thought. Dad was quiet, almost shy, and she could tell by the look on his face when he was about to say something important. She'd cut him off with a comment of her own before he could say a word. She knew he was too kind to say anything bad about Mom. He'd rather say nothing at all than something mean, but Laura wasn't ready for him to say anything whatsoever about the situation.

The prospect of eating pizza at Tony's with Dad, the way she and he and Mom had done almost every week of her life, made her chest feel tight. But once they were seated at their table, she relaxed. She talked about school and her recital. Didn't say a word about Mom's leaving. For a while, Dad just listened, but then he laid his hand on hers. "You saw your mom on Tuesday after school, said goodbye and all, right?" Laura nodded quickly. He patted her hand and said, "I'm sorry, baby. I'm so sorry." They finished their pizza in silence. She wasn't sure that was a good thing, but she was relieved. *We'll talk some other time.*

Laura felt a glimmer of anticipation on Sunday morning. *Mom and Dad are going to see each other today.* She sat on a high stool in her aunts' living room as Susie plaited her hair into a French braid.

"Should I tie on a ribbon?" her aunt asked as she finished up.

"No, the red elastic is good." Laura ran to the dressing table in the bedroom and checked out the braid with a hand mirror. "Thank you, Aunt Susie. You did a nice job. Just the way Mom does."

Susie stepped back and appraised her work. "Hmm. Maybe not quite as well as Carla does, but I came close."

"You like Mom, don't you?"

"Mm-hmm. I do."

"Why does Aunt Elaine hate her?"

"Oh, it's complicated. It's not really hatred. More a kind of jealousy. Elaine's a stubborn one. Can't let go of things. She felt like your mom came along with her sexy brown eyes and her cleavage and stole Stanley away from us."

"But he was a grown-up. He was going to fall in love and marry someone."

"Yeah, but like I said, it's complicated."

"That's what Mom says about Manny. About sex. Does sex make things complicated?"

"I'm not sure. Maybe it does." She hurried Laura out of the room with a wave of her hand. "Now you run downstairs and get dressed. Elaine and I'll meet you and Stanley at noon to walk over to the center."

Laura opened the front door and saw her dad in his dark gray suit and a white shirt facing the living room mirror. He turned and held up an olive green necktie. "What do you think? Is this a good color?"

If Mom were here, he'd be asking her. Her eyes would sparkle. "Oh Stan, I think the cobalt would be better." She'd rush into the bedroom and come back holding a bright blue tie. Tie it on him and turn him toward the mirror. "See, it brings out your eyes."

Laura studied the tie. It wasn't right—too dull—but she couldn't say that. "Yeah, the green's good. I'll get dressed while you put it on." As she watched her dad raise his collar and place the tie around his neck, she grasped at a slender strand of hope. *He's gonna see Mom this afternoon. Maybe he'll ask her to move back home.*

<hr />

Half an hour later, Laura peered from backstage at the people seated in the crowded hall. She didn't see Aunt Doreen and Mom. *They'd want to be in front. Maybe they got here late and had to sit at the back.*

When her turn came, Laura played "Clair De Lune" without a single mistake. She bowed the way Mrs. Friedman had taught them, then perused the audience. When she saw Doreen in the back row, sitting alone, her heart started to pound. *What if something has happened to Mom?*

After the recital, people gathered around telling her she'd done a beautiful job. That she'd sounded like a professional. Even Aunt Elaine bobbed her head in a satisfied way. *Don't they notice that Mom's not here? Isn't anyone worried?*

Stan stood apart from the chattering group, contemplating the lost look on Laura's face. More than anything, he wished he could tell her everything was going to work out, but he couldn't do that. He didn't believe it himself. He nodded at Doreen and tapped Laura's shoulder. "Aunt Doreen wants to take you for a soda to celebrate your performance. You go on. She'll drop you back at home in time for dinner." He watched the two of them walk out of the center. His usually energetic daughter was listless, her eyes downcast. She'd looked proud and excited when she stood up to take her bow, but disappointment and panic swept across her face as she searched the audience for her mom. *Carla let her down,* he thought. *We both did.*

Five minutes later Doreen unlocked the passenger door of her old Ford. Laura got in and burst into tears. "Where's Mom? Is she okay?"

"Honey, she wanted to come, but she didn't want to see all the people who knew she'd had to move out. She couldn't bear to face Elaine again.

And she was worried that you might be embarrassed by her. Your mom's real sensitive."

"Mom could never embarrass me. She's kind and beautiful. And the most wonderful mother in the world."

"She is a good mother, and she loves you. But she's in a tough spot. It'll take her a while to get her act together."

Laura leaned her forearms on her thighs and looked down at her hands. "Yeah, I understand."

"She left a little gift for you at my place. Let's go over there and talk."

Doreen didn't speak during the fifteen-minute drive or the walk up three flights of stairs to her apartment. *I've said enough. She needs some space. Time to process her feelings.* She took a ginger ale from the fridge and set it on the red laminate table in front of Laura, who managed a nod of thanks. It broke her heart to see the usually high-spirited girl so despondent. She handed her an envelope addressed in Carla's graceful, flowing hand and adorned with a garland of ivy drawn in green ink. "Here you go."

Laura pulled out a note, and read aloud, "I love you, sweetie. I hold you in my heart always. Mom."

"And here's your present," Doreen said.

Laura undid the bow of white satin ribbon tied around a package wrapped in shiny pink paper. Inside the small box was a medal on a chain. She picked up the necklace and studied the medallion. "It says *Saint Therese Pray For Us*. It's a Catholic thing. Is it okay for a person like me, who's not a Catholic, to wear it?"

Doreen was hazy on the guidelines regarding religious medals. She improvised, "Oh yeah. Anyone can. If you do, St. Therese'll watch over you—protect you. At least that's what the nuns taught your mom and me. Carla still thinks about all that stuff. Me, not so much. I know one thing though. Wearing it can't hurt." She opened the tiny latch and hung the chain around Laura's neck.

"Will you tell me stories about Mom? About when she was young?"

"Well, she was an artist when she was a girl. She could draw anything, absolutely true to life. If she'd gone to art school, she'd probably be famous by now. Instead, she and I learned how to cut hair."

"Haircutting is a kind of art, isn't it?" Doreen shrugged, and Laura kept talking. "Tell me about how Mom got on Dad's bus, and he was so handsome, she fell in love the second she saw him."

"You've heard that story a hundred times."

"Yeah, it's my favorite." She paused and her face clouded over. "Aunt Elaine says Dad and I weren't exciting enough for Mom. Is that true? Did Mom get bored with Dad and me?"

"No, Laura. She got bored with herself, not you and your dad. Maybe disappointed would be a better word than bored. She had so much talent, and she never got to use it."

"Did she blame Dad for the bankruptcy like Aunt Elaine says?"

"No, of course not. Your mom knew Stan was trying to do the right thing. He always does. He's a good man. Sad, but good."

"Do you think I'm going to grow up and be disappointed like Mom and sad like Dad?"

"No, you'll be happy. Everything's going to come up roses for you." Doreen's confident words belied doubts she couldn't quite dispel. "You're a smart girl. That's a fact. You passed the Hunter College Secondary School entrance exam with flying colors. Next fall you'll start seventh grade in the city, and the teachers there will prepare you to go on to college and be a success. We're all going to be proud and happy for you."

"Everyone?" Laura asked. Doreen nodded, and Laura frowned. "Even Aunt Elaine? You think she could be happy?"

"Yep, even Aunt Elaine. We're all going to be." She snapped her fingers. "Hey, I have a super idea. What's your dad's favorite dinner?"

"Beef stew with roasted vegetables."

"I've got potatoes and onions and carrots. And a chuck roast in the fridge. Let's make a stew and carry it over to your house in a covered dish. You and Stan can celebrate your recital and your happy future."

"Will you stay and eat with us?"

"No, I think it should be a father-daughter event. Just you and your dad. You two are going to be on your own now. You need to learn to care for each other without Carla. To be happy together." A moment passed before she added, "Okay?" That little question, which seemed an afterthought, actually went straight to the heart of the matter. Doreen sat waiting for a reply. All she got was silence.

Laura stared at the red table top, holding the satin ribbon in place with her left index finger while she smoothed it with her right. After several seconds, she picked it up and laid it in a loop on top of the folded wrapping paper. She walked slowly across the kitchen, humming "Clair De Lune," then turned to face Doreen. "Okay, I'll help make the stew." She raised her index finger. "But you'll have to cut up the meat. I don't know how. And I'm going to need a brush to scrub the carrots and potatoes." She grinned. "Dad doesn't like them peeled."

Laura's tone banished the cloud of uncertainty that had hovered over Doreen for most of the week. She took an easy breath. *She's going to survive this. We all will. We're going to be fine.* "You got it, honey." She pointed at the cupboard below the sink. "The vegetable brush is on a hook right inside that door."

A PRECIOUS SEASON

1988

The sky over Tompkins County had just begun to lighten when Andrew Campbell opened his eyes. He lay still and let the June morning settle in around him, for about a minute, then sat up with a start. *God, I almost forgot. I'm working with Dad this morning. He'll want to be on the road by five thirty.*

High winds had toppled a couple of trees in Brendan Thorne's orchard, and he'd offered the Campbells all the wood they wanted if they did the cutting. Mark, Andrew's dad, called it a win-win. "Brendan gets his orchard cleaned up, and we get some beautiful firewood and a workout. You and I can cut and split all the wood in half a day."

His dad cracked open the bedroom door. "Andrew, you awake?"

"Yeah, barely."

"Change of plans, son. I'm going to be tied up most of the day. We can postpone the job. Or, if you'd like, you can drive the truck over and work on your own today. Cut all the wood and split us a cord. The bed won't hold a full cord so you'll have to make a second trip."

"Oh yeah, I can do that."

"Great. They're saying it's going to reach eighty degrees by noon. You'll want to get an early start."

"I'll be ready in five." It was Andrew's first summer with a driver's license, and he was up for any job that required driving the F-250. He pulled on jeans and a tee shirt, laced his boots, and headed downstairs. He wolfed some scrambled eggs, kissed his mother, and took the lunch she handed him. "Thanks, Mom." The screen door banged behind him.

His dad stood waiting by the '85 Ford. "I called the Thornes. They're expecting you. You can pull in on the northeast corner of the orchard and get right to work." Andrew loaded the chain saw and splitting maul onto the bed of the truck. As he was about to leap up into the cab, his dad stopped him. "I know you're raring to go, but it's going to be chilly for another hour or so. You'd best put on a long-sleeved shirt."

"Oh yeah." Andrew ran to the porch and grabbed one from a hook. *He's right. I'm stoked.*

Andrew glanced at his watch. Two thirty. Unrelenting sun poured over his shirtless back. *The weatherman was right on. This is the hottest day we've had.* He paused to wipe the sweat from his face and was back at work in an instant. *I'll be lucky to finish this job before dinner.*

Between the sharp cracks of wood splitting, a voice rang out, "Hi, I come bearing lemonade." Andrew looked up and saw a dark-haired girl in cutoff jeans and a blue and white tube top approaching. She set a red

Coleman jug and a glass on the ground and stepped toward him with an outstretched hand. "I'm Jessie Thorne. My mom says you've been out here since six. She thought you could use an ice-cold drink."

He put the maul down and pulled on his tee shirt. He didn't have time to socialize, but he took her hand. "Yeah, thanks. I'm Andrew Campbell."

"Wow. David's little brother is all grown up." She fastened her eyes on his. "How old are you?"

"Almost seventeen . . . How do you know David?"

"In other words, you're sixteen. Nothing wrong with admitting that." She bit her lip and smiled. "I spent a lot of time with him a couple of summers ago. I was about your age. I called it *almost seventeen* too." She tipped her head to the side. "I bet you like the Beatles."

"Yeah, I do. I've listened to their music my whole life. My dad's a major fan."

"I know. David told me. So-o . . . sixteen . . . you probably have a girlfriend."

"Not really . . . David told you Dad played the Beatles? I didn't think he paid attention to stuff like that. So what kind of relationship did you have with him anyway? Was he your boyfriend?"

"How could David have spent his whole childhood listening to the Beatles without noticing?" Her voice went soft, almost drifted away. "No, not my boyfriend. He seemed too big for this little part of the world. He sure was sweet to me though." And then she was back. "So, you don't have a girlfriend? Hmm. What do you like to do when you're not cutting wood?"

She's flirting with me. Andrew was flattered. *And making fun of me.* It rattled him. He filled a glass and chugged the cold lemonade. "Well, for one thing, I like drinking iced beverages." He set the glass on the ground and picked up the maul. "I've gotta get back to work."

"Yeah, of course. Say hi to David for me when you see him."

"Sure. Would you like him to call you?" He tried to gauge her reaction, but she wasn't giving anything away.

She bent to collect the jug and empty glass, then faced him. "No. But you can. I'd like that." She backed away for a few paces. He watched her turn and saunter across the clearing.

No way I'm going to call her. Fuck. I don't compete with David. He stood a log on end, raised the maul overhead, and dropped it dead center. *Perfect. Physical labor is one area where I outshine him—maybe.*

Andrew had worked with his parents at the Ithaca Farmers Market since childhood. This year, for the first time, their farm's weekend stands were his responsibility—from loading the truck at seven in the morning to closing up at three. Strong and efficient, he liked the physical work, but what he loved was dealing with customers, sharing the fruits of his family's labor.

On the third Saturday in June, music drifted up from the waterfront and the buzz of human exuberance filled the air. Amidst stands heaped with multi-colored produce, Andrew was working double-time to keep up with the clamor for strawberries, peas, and his mom's flowers.

Jessie showed up at noon. She pointed at a carton of strawberries. "I want those." Then held up a canvas tote. "And you can give me two baskets of peas."

Andrew smiled. Handed her the strawberries and dumped the peas into her bag. "You got it. That'll be eight dollars."

She gave him a ten. "So you do have a smile. Is it just for customers?"

"Actually, I smile quite a lot."

"Good. It's a nice one. If you're not busy after you finish today, we could walk downtown together. Okay?"

"Uhh . . . yeah, sure. Come back about three."

Jessie disappeared into the throng, and Andrew turned to the next customer. For the next three hours, he sold peas and irises and peonies and answered questions about strawberries, but his mind was on her. *Wow.* She was almost nineteen. She was beautiful. *Wow.*

She appeared as he loaded the last crate onto the truck. "You're all packed up. I wanted to help." She shrugged. "Oh well, maybe next time."

Half an hour later they sat under a tree in DeWitt Park eating ice cream. "In the last twenty minutes you've smiled a half dozen times and laughed out loud twice," Jessie said. "Quite a change from that stern, serious almost seventeen-year-old splitting wood in my dad's orchard. What's up? Which one is the real Andrew?"

"I was working that day."

"Not a good explanation. You were working today. I watched you for ten minutes before I bought my produce. You never stopped smiling."

"Okay. The truth? I could tell you were making fun of me, laughing at me. You made me uncomfortable."

"I wasn't laughing at you. I was smiling. You were so serious you couldn't tell the difference."

"If I was so dull and serious, what made you come looking for me today?"

She licked her ice cream. "Your body."

She was flirting again. He tried for a nonchalant expression, but a laugh escaped. "I'm not David—nothing like him. If you're looking to have a summer like you had with him, I'm-"

"Oh my god. I knew in a minute you weren't like David. And I don't want to recapture that summer—just enjoy the rest of this one. I suspected you might have a sense of humor hiding somewhere. That's why I sought you out today." She leaned against the tree and giggled. "But your body is a bonus."

⬥

"Andrew, Jessie called before you got up," Jane Campbell said at breakfast the following Saturday. "She'll be working with her dad this afternoon. Won't be ready until about eight."

"Thanks, Mom, but in the future I'd like you to wake me if she calls before I get up."

David set his coffee cup on the table and faced Andrew. "Jessie? Jessie Thorne?"

"Yeah."

"Damn, you're playing in the big leagues, bro. Watch out."

"I can take care of myself."

"Okay." David held out his hands and shrugged. "So how do you and Jessie spend your time?"

"I've only been with her twice. We just hang out."

"Did you hear that, Mom? Dad? He's barely old enough for a driver's license. He *hangs out* with an older woman. I wonder-"

Jane interjected, "David, stop it. You don't know what it's like to have a big brother teasing you. Ha! Older woman? She must be all of nineteen. Andrew, ignore your brother. You go ahead and hang out."

"I'm fine." He threw David a sidelong frown. "I don't let him get to me. But speaking of driving, I would like to use your car tonight, Mom."

As they walked away from the table, David laid his hand on Andrew's shoulder. "Sorry. Your seeing Jessie took me by surprise, that's all."

"Yeah, whatever."

"It's great. I mean it—she's a nice girl. Be sweet to her."

Andrew turned away without a word. *What's that all about?* Those first words about Jessie, "You're playing in the big leagues," were classic David—taunting, knowing. But, "Be sweet to her," wasn't the kind of advice Andrew expected from him. And the words mirrored Jessie's. "He sure was sweet to me." *I wonder what kind of relationship they had that summer.* She'd seemed cryptic the day in the orchard, but she was actually pretty open. *I'll ask her tonight.*

Jessie's plan for the evening included a walk up Stewart Avenue to the north end of campus and back down. She spent nine months a year at school in Colorado. "I stay in condition for Denver by walking to the top of this hill most days and hiking the gorge trails three or four times a week throughout the summer." She set the pace. Way too fast for talking. They circled the museum of art and walked across the slope to a bench facing the sunset before Andrew spoke.

"I said hi to David from you this morning." He hadn't actually, but it seemed like a good conversation starter. "I've been wondering if he ever took you to the farm? I never saw you together."

"A few times. I saw you, a skinny kid out in the woods, watching birds or bugs or something. David called you mother nature's son."

"Damn, he did listen to Dad's music. I never thought he did. By the way, I still watch birds and bugs."

"But you're not a skinny kid."

"Yeah, I guess not. Tell me about you and David. If you weren't an item, what'd you guys do that summer?"

"I didn't say we weren't an item. I said he wasn't my boyfriend . . . I wasn't his girlfriend. He already had one, but she was in London for the summer. They were both free to see other people for twelve weeks, and I was his other person. O-oh . . . we did a lot."

"So you weren't his girlfriend, but you slept together?"

"Yeah, we did. Does that bother you?"

"I guess not. I think it might have bothered him—or you."

"No, not at all. It was all above board and honest. He stopped by our place one afternoon to return a chipper your dad had borrowed. I'd just finished eleventh grade at St. Mary's Academy, and he was this sophisticated Princeton student. But we clicked. He was a wonderful first lover—tender, gentle, patient."

Andrew definitely did not want to hear about Jessie's sex with David, but he wondered what role the relationship might be playing in her present life. "So you came out to the orchard that day to see if the skinny kid had grown into another David?"

"No, I went out to see what his brother was like. No one, not even my boyfriend, Jason, whom I love dearly, will be another David."

"What? You have a boyfriend? How does he fit into your summer program?"

"He doesn't. I already told you. I want to have fun. Don't you?"

He ignored her question and continued asking his own. "And the boyfriend you love so much? What will he be doing?"

"Having fun at home in San Diego. This open summer was his idea, not mine. I guess he wants to fool around before he decides to really settle down."

"And you? If you want to fool around, I may not be your best option."

"I don't want to fool around. I want the two of us to have a good time and see where we end up."

Her words made no sense to Andrew. Either she was misleading him or he was misreading her. "When I said I was nothing like my brother, I was trying to tell you something. Remember how you said he was too big for this place? Well, I'm not. I'm exactly the right size for it. Two years after not being David's girlfriend, you're still—I don't know— raving about him. Not that I want to compete with him. No way. Fuck, I couldn't if I wanted to." He paused for a breath. "For all I know, you're trying to get him back through me."

"Andrew, I flirted with you the day we met because you appealed to me. When I said I didn't want David to call me, I meant it. I'm an honest person."

"I'm sorry, but I don't get it. Why would a girl like you want to hang out with a kid like me?"

She began to speak slowly, carefully. "I wasn't planning to be . . . explicit, but maybe I have to be. I don't expect you to play David's role. I want to be your . . . mentor." For a moment she was silent, then her words tumbled out. "That day in the orchard when you chugged the glass of lemonade and picked up the splitting maul, I saw something solid in you. I wanted to see more of it." She touched his hand. "Listen. If we end up taking walks and eating ice cream for the next two months, it'll be okay with me. But I think we'll do more than that. You find out what you want. I'll try to lead you. Will you trust me?"

Andrew sat, speechless, too bewildered to answer.

She searched his face. "Do you like me?" He could tell she was dead serious.

"You know I do."

"Are you in love with me?"

"I-I-" He paused. "No. I don't think so."

"Good. And you won't fall in love with me?"

"How can I be sure?"

She kissed his cheek. "You can't. Let's go get an ice cream."

———————

For three weeks, Andrew's life followed a pattern. Eight hours of work, seven days a week, followed by evenings with Jessie. He gave her wildlife lessons as they hiked "because nature is for more than exercise."

And she taught him to play squash "because everyone should know how to play at least one ballgame." They shared popcorn at the summer's blockbusters and bonded while they laughed at Tom Hanks and Jamie Leigh Curtis and Michael Keaton.

Friday night of the third week was a turning point. *Bull Durham*, a film about sex and baseball, was playing. All Andrew saw was the sex. Afterward, they sat in the driveway of his parents' house in Jessie's car. He touched her face, traced her cheekbone. His kiss was tentative. Her response wasn't. Ten minutes later, she pulled away. "Andrew, we should stop." She gently pushed him out of the car. "We'll finish this another time."

"What?" Everything was a blur. "When? Tomorrow?"

"Sunday, after the market. There's a rundown garden house between the orchard and the woods on the west side of our property. I cleaned it up a little, in case we wanted to use it. Okay?"

He took a deep breath, cleared his head. "Yeah. Good. I was wondering where we'd go. This Triumph doesn't even have a back seat, and using my mom's car would feel so wrong."

At work on Sunday Andrew had to shake himself to attention more than once. He kept going over his plan. *Pack up, drive to the farm, unload, shower.* If his parents were home, he'd try to act normal. *Jesus, how am I going to do that?* He looked at his watch every few minutes. One final look. Three o'clock. He put his head down and got to work. Completed the familiar closing up tasks on autopilot.

He started the truck, put the Beatles' *Blue Album* in the cassette player, and fast-forwarded to "Hey Jude." The words of the song carried him all the way to the farm. His mom's car was gone. He breathed a sigh of relief and unloaded the empty crates. Carried a basket of beans into the kitchen, and headed for the shower. Fifteen minutes later he was on the road, driving in a daze that persisted until he jumped from the cab, and the slam of the truck's door stopped the thrum in his head.

Jessie, her hair falling in a cascade of dark waves over one shoulder, waited in the garden house wearing a pale yellow dress. Andrew's heart banged. He pulled off his shirt and took a quick breath. *Here goes.*

She unbuttoned the dress, let it drop to the floor, and he reached around to unhook her bra. "One hand," she whispered as she slid his other one down her belly. He kissed her once, and she took over—guiding him with her hands, her lips, her breath. She walked him to a rattan daybed and sat beside him. "Lie back." She bathed him in the perfume of her sweat, surrounded him with herself, and they moved in rhythm with each other until they collapsed together. Spent.

Jessie rolled over and laid her head on Andrew's shoulder. "You were fantastic."

"No-o. You were."

"Okay, we both were."

***

The pattern changed. They still hiked or swam and sat in the park eating ice cream at the end of their work days. But when the sun set, they decamped to the orchard and walked through the patch of wild bergamot that led to the garden house. They'd throw open the dilapidated French doors and make love in the blue twilight.

David came home for a weekend in August. Helped Andrew load the Ford on Sunday morning and drove his Tacoma to the market at three to pack up. "Dad says you've been working overtime this summer. Take the rest of the day off. I'll haul everything back to the farm." He didn't drop a hint or cast a knowing look. Didn't say a word about Jessie.

Andrew watched him drive off. *What do you know? He's actually decent.*

***

On Friday of Jessie's last week in town, Andrew picked her up at six o'clock. "I've made a plan. My friend Finn's aunt has a cottage on Skaneateles Lake. She's away for the month, and he's house sitting. He's going to clear out and let us stay there tonight. I told Mom and Dad I'd be staying with him. I really want to watch you sleep, okay?"

"Way more than okay. That's one of the nicest wishes about me I've ever heard. We can take turns watching each other." She patted his thigh. "You've made outstanding progress. Two months ago, who could have imagined Andrew Campbell arranging a dirty weekend?"

"What do you mean *dirty?*"

"It's a term for a sexual get-away."

"Hmm. I don't really like the expression. I was aiming for romantic."

"You're not going all starry-eyed on me, are you?"

"Maybe a little." He grinned. "Nah, not really."

An hour later, they sat on a deck that stretched over the glittering lake, eating tomatoes and Italian bread. They watched the water go from blue to gold to gray and finally black, then stepped inside and felt their way through the unlit house. When Andrew reached out in search of a wall switch, Jessie grasped his hand. "No lights. This night is magic. Don't break the spell."

The next morning, she lay asleep on a square of white sunlight in the center of the bed—her dark hair tousled, her mascara smudged—with the rumpled sheet a tangle around her tanned legs. He watched transfixed until she opened her eyes and smiled up at him. "You wake up happy," he said, "so do I. You don't get to watch me though. I've been up since before dawn."

"I won't get to see you wake up, but I did watch you sleep. Last night. The moon shone in all silver, and you lay on your back without moving. It was eerie how still you were." She sat up. "Today's our first morning together and our last day. The summer's been a success, hasn't it?"

"Yeah, even better than you promised."

"And you didn't fall in love with me."

"Yeah, no, I didn't. I can't imagine why not. You're the coolest girl I've ever known."

She gave a little shrug. "It turned out the way it was supposed to. It's over. We'll say goodbye in an hour. Tomorrow I'll fly back to Colorado." Her voice went soft like on that first day in the orchard. "And this summer will be a lovely memory."

"I'll write you."

"No." She shook her head. "You can't prolong this precious season. Hold it in your heart until you meet the right girl, one who'll share your whole life, who won't be a secret. Someday we'll see each other in a store or at a restaurant in town, and we'll smile, even hug each other. Like old friends."

Andrew had been perfectly content until that very moment, but Jessie's words brought tears to his eyes. She wiped his face and took hold of his shoulders. "Like old friends, right?"

He didn't have a clue about the future, but he knew what she needed to hear. "Sure, if we see each other again, that's what we'll do." He leaned over and kissed the top of her head. *Maybe she's right. She has been about everything so far.*

BEAUTIFUL GIRL

1990

It was 8 a.m. the second Monday of summer holiday, and Greg had just finished mixing flour with yeast and water for bread when the phone sounded. He looked at the little screen, *quite an innovation, this caller ID*. He liked knowing who was trying to reach him. The name that flashed was unexpected—his wife's. She wouldn't call during her work day unless an emergency had come up. "Carolyn, what is it?"

"Something's happened."

"I assumed that. What?"

"It's Sophie. She's in a very bad way. She called in tears-"

"She called you at work? She knows I'm on holiday. Why didn't she call here?"

"She said she was afraid to talk to you; she-"

"Afraid—of me? Christ, what's going on?"

"She didn't sleep at all last night. What she's calling fear is a confusing combination of emotions. She and Matt have split up after a number of incidents of physical violence on his part and violent anger on hers. He left for good yesterday morning. I'm relieved about that, but Sophie's in a rough place emotionally. I have patients until three this afternoon. I think you should drive to London and bring her home for a while, maybe for good."

"O-oh my god." The image of their daughter alone and in pain overwhelmed him; he stood silent.

"Greg? Greg?"

"Yes, of course, I'll do that. Is she safe by herself in the flat?"

"Yes. All she needs right now is to be with someone she loves, who loves her. I've told her you'll be there by noon. She's expecting you."

Greg looked around the room—a sticky mass of dough on the flour covered counter, an oiled bowl awaiting the bread he'd been about to knead, and a sudsy sink full of measuring cups and spoons ready for washing up. "Okay, I'm leaving the kitchen as is. You can take care of it when you get home. By the way, should I call Will? He could catch a train and be at her flat within an hour."

"No, no. She's not ready to see Will."

He took off his apron, grabbed a jacket and his car keys, was on the road within minutes. Full of care, but not anxious. He knew Sophie wasn't about to harm herself. Carolyn, a therapist attuned by temperament and training to discern each note in the affective symphony of a conversation, had said their daughter was safe. *She is not suicidal. She's needy, and what she needs is family. She needs me.*

Sophie had never been afraid of him—or anything—in her life. Will was their tender child. Quiet and, if anything, overly empathic. More than once, he'd avoided expressing himself to Greg because he didn't "want to hurt Dad's feelings." Sophie never felt slighted herself so she never gave potential hurt feelings a thought. Said exactly what was on her mind. She was joyful and generous and courageous. Headstrong at times, but all in all, an easy child.

Not such an easy adult. A year ago, following her second year at university, she had gone to Madrid for eight weeks of study. She fell in love with Matt, who was there on holiday before starting a job as an investment banker in London. Suddenly Sophie's plan to one day teach literature no longer held any appeal. There was no reasoning with her. She opted out of third year and moved in with Matt. He was bright and charming, a bit smooth for Greg's taste, but apparently what their daughter needed at the moment. He and Carolyn had expected the flame would die out within a few months, but to their surprise, Sophie called in February to announce she was pregnant, that she and Matt were getting married at the beginning of March.

Carolyn had hung up the phone and shaken her head in disbelief. She looked solemnly at Greg. "Is that what we did? No pregnancy, but did we shock our parents when we got married five weeks after I visited Yorkshire for the first time?"

Greg smiled. "Maybe yours, not mine. I'd been preparing them for months."

Sophie miscarried in April. At the end of a tearful call, she whispered, "Matt thinks losing the baby is for the best."

Greg couldn't have guessed how one year would change their exuberant daughter. *Sophie's abandoned her studies, married the wrong man, suffered a miscarriage, and now sits alone and desperately sad in a London flat.* Carolyn, who worked with traumatized wives and who never over-reacted, considered Sophie's state serious enough for Greg to drop everything and drive four hours to collect her.

———————

Despite heavy late morning traffic in central London, he reached St. George's Drive at noon and walked four blocks through the glorious midday to Sophie's flat, where the curtains were drawn tight against the brilliant sunshine. He rang the bell and announced, "Sophie, it's Dad."

She opened the door dressed in a rumpled tracksuit, her dark hair unbrushed, eyes downcast to avoid his.

He opened his arms. "Sophie, Sophie." She fell against him, and her sobs tore at his heart. "Oh my dear, dear girl. Let's go inside."

They sat silently, holding hands, until Greg said, "I know you're miserable. Your mother would know how to start this conversation, but I don't, so I'm going to wait for you. You take as much time as you want—to cry, to talk, whatever you need to do."

"Okay, Dad." When at last she raised her head and looked directly at him, he noticed a bruise under her left eye.

"Oh, Sophie, I love you so."

Her hand shook as she touched the purple skin of her cheek. "I'm ashamed. So ashamed. How could I grow up in a home with a wonderful, gentle father like you and fall in love with a man like Matt?"

"We don't get to choose the person we fall in love with."

"Mum chose you. She had another boyfriend and she left him because you were a better person."

He frowned. "Did your mum tell you that?"

"Not really, but I know that's what she did."

Greg shook his head. "You're wrong. She left him because she didn't love him. She loved me. We were lucky. Maybe with Matt, you were unlucky, but that's not shameful."

"He says it's my fault that he hits me and sleeps with other women. That I tricked him with my pregnancy, trapped him, and now he's angry and needs to be free."

"That sounds like an excuse to me."

"Maybe, but I have done things. Things you wouldn't approve of. I-" She sobbed. "I-"

Greg interrupted, "You don't have to confess, not to me. I've done things I regret. Everyone has. No confession unless you feel you must."

"I do. That is what I feel." She looked down at her lap. "But it's a selfish feeling. I want you to listen and then say you love me no matter what I've done."

"So no confession needed. I will love you no matter what you've done. Now, I'm going to open some curtains and put the kettle on. You go wash your face and get ready for tea."

He turned on the water and opened the refrigerator. "I see you have milk. Where do you keep the biscuits?"

She called from the bathroom, "In the cupboard to the right of the window. I'll help."

"No, not today. Just sit at the table and wait." He laid out cups and spoons and sugar and milk and biscuits. "I can handle tea. I'm the one who taught you, remember? If there'd been time to find it before I left home this morning, I'd have brought my *Revolver* album to accompany me, like old times, eh?" Sophie managed a smile.

They sat quietly for a while, drinking and eating as if they were a happy father and daughter, until Greg said, "I do need to know your plans. Have you and Matt talked about the future?"

She scoffed. "You mean like you and Mum would do? No, we've screamed and cursed each other. When he left yesterday morning, he said he wanted me out of the flat for good by Friday. It's only fair. He's the one who pays for everything." She paused and continued in a shaky voice, "He taunted me as he walked down the hall toward the front door. Said he knew I'd call my . . . uptight Yorkshire parents. That it was my only option because two years at university and a summer of partying in Madrid hardly made me employable . . . And that you wouldn't take me back if you knew half of what I've done this past year. That's why I need to-"

"Sophie, stop, right now. There'll be time to tell us everything you want us to know, but not now. Let's get what you're going to take and start packing the car."

They were quiet for the first half hour of the drive north. Every once in a while, Greg would reach out and squeeze Sophie's hand, and she'd say, "Thanks, Dad."

As they turned onto the M1, he said, "Your brother's totally unaware of what you're going through. He's going to find out at some point."

"I know. I told Mum not to tell him yet. It's just that he's so good, and I'm not anymore. Not good and not brave. I couldn't face telling you, so Mum did. Maybe you could be the one to tell Will. Would you?"

"Of course."

An hour later, Sophie cleared her throat. "I know you said no confession, but I have to get some things off my chest. Would you mind if I did that now, before we see Mum?"

"You don't owe either of us an explanation, but you may tell me whatever you wish, whenever you're ready."

"Okay . . . firstly, I have to admit my whole reason for going to Madrid was a lie. It wasn't to learn Spanish. I just wanted to escape the monotony of Yorkshire." Greg smiled and nodded. "I met Matt the day I got there, and all we did was party from midnight till dawn for two months. Then we moved to London and continued our wild lifestyle. Saying we drank to excess would be an understatement." Greg nodded again. "We were wilder than you and Mum could imagine." She took a quick breath. "He used cocaine, and so did I, a lot."

"I believe you underestimate your mum's and my ability to imagine."

"And there's more. I gave up all the drugs and alcohol when I found out I was pregnant, but I started drinking again after I lost the baby. I drink myself to sleep every night . . . I'm an alcoholic."

"Perhaps. Your mum has seen quite a bit of that in her practice. If you need help, she'll know where to find it."

"You think I'm going to be all right." Sophie's voice was full of wonder. "I can tell that's what you think."

"I know you will be. It won't be easy, but if you can tolerate your *uptight* Yorkshire parents, we'll be there to lean on for as long as you need us. And when you don't, we'll step back."

"O-oh, Dad." She laughed out loud. Then cried, ragged sobs that continued until her head dropped back against the seat. At last, she slept.

Greg listened to the quiet breathing of his first born child and wished her "a sleep full of sweet dreams." *When she wakes, the work will start, and it will be the hardest work she's ever undertaken.* He touched her shoulder and whispered, "My beautiful girl."

STANDING ON THE
THRESHOLD

1992

Gloria Levin looked at her watch. Two forty-five. She opened a folder and reread the notes that accompanied the application of Ellinor O'Neal, the new student she was about to meet. Excellent references from teachers. They called her a thoughtful student of superior intellect who led by example. Straight As. Excellent AP scores. 5s in World History and English Literature and Composition. 4s in Calculus and Physics. Literary works studied in class or read on her own spanned the breadth of the western canon. Her application essay began with the sentence, "I grew up in a 'bee-loud glade.' "

The words of the story she recounted—of an unconventional childhood spent savoring the glories of nature and listening to the poetry of Shakespeare and Yeats—had been underlined, starred, and studded with remarks by its various readers: *Astute, Stunning imagery, An eloquent memoir.* The essay, along with recommendations and grade reports, composed an impressive record of a fortunate girl, but a letter sent by her high school counselor cast a shadow across the glowing resume.

November 1, 1991

Office of Undergraduate Admissions, Hunter College

New York City

To Whom It May Concern:

I am writing to inform you of a tragedy in the life of Ellinor O'Neal, a senior at Cremona High School who has applied for acceptance through early decision for a place in the Fall 1992 freshman class. A month ago her father and fourteen-year-old brother died in a fire. Having access to her academic records, you know she is an excellent student, a remarkable girl. She's doing an admirable job of keeping up with her classwork and plans to begin her first year of study next fall. However, as one would expect, she is devastated by what she is experiencing and must cancel the on-campus interview scheduled for November 12. I will keep you apprised of her progress.

Sincerely,

Marianne Lawton, Counselor

Cremona High School,

Cremona, NY 13151

Before closing the folder, Gloria reread a letter sent by the Dean of Students informing Ellinor that a face-to-face interview would not be required. *Today is her first time on campus. This appointment with me is her introduction to Hunter.* She slid the file aside and tapped her index finger on the desk. She felt anxious about meeting the young woman whose grievous loss had undoubtedly altered what should have been a happy and exciting experience. She looked at her watch again. 2:58.

———◆———

Ellie had caught the bus in Syracuse at eight thirty that morning and arrived at the Port Authority Terminal in New York at one fifteen. A year ago she would have been filled with happy anticipation to step from the bus into one of the world's great cities, but losing her dad and brother had altered her. Sapped the vitality from her. She wasn't setting out on an adventure. She was fulfilling an obligation. She had to get to Hunter College by three.

Her mom, a reference librarian, had studied the New York City transit system and helped her make a plan before she left home. It had seemed so easy that morning—she would simply follow the signs that pointed to Grand Central Station. But as she looked up at the dizzying array of signs and arrows, she was baffled. She had no idea how to get the right subway. *I can't do this on my own,* she thought as she scanned the crowd for a friendly face. She caught the eye of a girl wearing a dark blue headscarf. "I want to take a subway to Grand Central Station. Do you know where I should go?" She paused. "And I don't have a ticket. I need one, don't I?"

The girl replied in accented, but understandable, English. "Single ride?"

Ellie shrugged. "I guess so."

"Okay, follow me." She pointed. "You walk that way for a block until you get to Times Square. Buy a pass at the machine to get through the turnstile. You catch the 7 train—just two stops—to Grand Central Station. Do you know where you're going from there?"

"Yes, to East 68th Street."

"Okay," the girl thought for a few seconds. "Then you catch the 6. You have to read signs. Can you do that on your own?"

"Yes. Thank you. Thank you so much."

"No problem. You be careful."

"I will." A whisper of optimism rose up in Ellie. *What a good person. She's a foreigner. Maybe someone helped her when she was lost, and now she's done the same for me.* She walked up 41st Avenue and bought a pass at Times Square Station. She stood in the waiting throng, then boarded the train. For the first time in her life, she had traveled beyond the Finger Lakes. Ready or not, she would have to confront the venture that was unfolding before her.

The three knocks on Gloria's door were tentative. "Come on in." The girl from the photo entered. Long, wavy blonde hair and blue eyes. But her face was thinner, and her smile looked forced. Gloria stood up. "I'm Professor Levin. You must be Ellinor."

"Yes. I actually go by Ellie."

"Fine, Ellie. And I actually go by Gloria." She shook Ellie's hand and gestured toward a chair. "Put your bags down and have a seat."

"Thank you. I'm pleased to meet you."

"And we're pleased to have you here. I'm speaking for all my colleagues when I say we want you to feel comfortable at Hunter. If you need anything, if you have a question, just ask."

"Yes, I will."

"You're standing on the threshold of the future—one you'll both discover and create. It's going to be an exciting time."

"I'm sure I'll be happy here." She sounded polite, but not at all sure.

"We have counseling services if you ever feel the need to talk."

A look of alarm crossed the girl's face. The forced smile returned, and she swallowed. "Thank you."

Gloria sucked in her breath. The comment about counseling had been unnecessary—a blunder. She quickly added, "It's a service available to all of our students," then changed tack and continued. "I see from your records that you're a literature lover. I happen to share your enthusiasm for Yeats."

Ellie's posture—her whole demeanor—changed. Her face lit up. "I've never had a teacher who loved Yeats. My mom does, so we read it together, but I've never shared Yeats with a teacher. Maybe I can take a class from you sometime."

"That would be nice. I think we'd both enjoy it." She pointed at Ellie's bags. "I'm guessing you haven't moved in yet. Do you know how to get to your residence?"

"Yes, it's not far. Just on 79th Street."

"Are you comfortable going there on your own?"

"Oh, yeah. They're expecting me." She hesitated. "I should probably get going if that's okay with you."

"Of course. It's been a pleasure talking to you. Feel free to stop by any time."

"Yes, thank you for . . . for welcoming me to college." She walked out of the office, blew out a breath of relief, and mentally checked off one of the day's tasks.

Ellie's favorite class was Shakespeare's Heroines. She had always been a good questioner, but with Professor Barnard's encouragement, everyone in the class was. The questions and answers that ricocheted about the room each Tuesday and Thursday morning exhilarated her. She'd never before been challenged to think so hard. *I'm getting a real education.*

The day she arrived in the city, after being helped by the girl at the Port Authority, Ellie had realized something. She hadn't asked anyone for help in almost a year, hadn't initiated any conversation whatsoever. She decided to try being more like she'd been before her dad and brother died—open with people, trusting. For two weeks, she talked with class-mates, even laughed at their jokes. But she wasn't trusting. She remained on guard, carefully avoiding the subject of family. *I'm not being open. I haven't let a single person in.* She vowed to leave her comfort zone. One day at lunch when a girl was talking about being an only child—how she'd always wanted a sibling—Ellie blurted out, "I have a brother," then took a jagged breath. "He died a year ago." After two or three murmurs of regret, interaction around the table came to a halt. No talk, no eye contact. *The truth about my family destroyed the conversation.*

The prospect of that scene recurring filled her with anxiety. She aban-doned her resolve to reach out. Concentrated on coursework and kept to herself outside of class. She would lie in bed each night, dreading the next day. Somewhere between wakefulness and sleep, the image of her brother dying in a fire would momentarily take her breath away; she'd squeeze her eyes tight to block the memory. When she began to breathe normally, she'd pray for something—she wasn't sure what—"Please, please, please."

Then one Saturday afternoon her life changed. She walked into the lounge at the end of her wing and startled a girl who lay stretched out on a sofa, eating dolmades and reading *A Moveable Feast*. The dark-eyed girl put her book down. "Hey, what's up?" She propped herself on an elbow, then swung her legs over the edge of the couch and twirled her hair into a knot. "I'm Laura." She pointed at a plate on the coffee table. "Do you like dolma? Even if you usually don't, you'll like these. My dad's Greek neighbor made them."

"I've never tasted dolma, good or bad." Ellie took one from the plate. "Mmm, it's delicious. Are you a Hemingway fan?"

"Absolutely not. Only this book. Someday I'll go to Paris." Her words gleamed with expectation. "I'll walk around to every place he writes about. I've never been to Paris. Have you?"

"No, I'm from the Finger Lakes. I've never been anywhere. This is as far from home as I've traveled."

"Wow. That's unreal. What's your family like? How did you end up here?"

Her manner was so unabashed and unguarded, that Ellie dropped her defenses. "I had a wonderful family, but it's shattered. My dad and my brother, Danny, died last year. Now my mom and I only have each other."

Tears filled Laura's eyes. She grabbed Ellie's shoulders and hugged her. "Oh, I'm so sorry." A minute later, she said, "I bet you haven't been to the Village yet. Do you want to go for a cappuccino?"

"Sure. I mean, it sounds good, but I've never had one."

"Then it's about time. Come on." They headed for the 72nd Street station. In twenty-five minutes they were sitting in an ancient coffee shop, and Laura was sharing her story.

She was unlike anyone Ellie'd ever met. When her parents got divorced, her mother moved to California, and she stayed in the Bronx with her dad. She was open about everything—her sex life, her dad's bankruptcy, her mom's affairs. After their coffee, they walked the whole way back to 79th Street—an hour and a half—and never stopped talking. They took turns. Laura talked about her parents. "When my mom moved all the way across the country, I thought I'd never be happy again, but it turned out okay. She made me promise I'd take care of Dad, and the more I tried, the better I felt. Dad and I cared for each other. We went to Shakespeare in the Park together every summer. Room by room, we painted our whole house. He even borrowed a car and taught me to drive." She took a breath. "I've only gone to visit Mom once, but she comes back home for a week every summer and stays with her friend Doreen. She and Dad and I always go for pizza. Even though their marriage didn't work out, they'll be linked forever." Her eyes shone. "Because they both love me."

Ellie bubbled over with praise for Danny. "He could sail any boat in any kind of weather. He built a raft that could carry six people across the lake when he was ten years-old. He was self-confident, but totally modest. He and I were nothing alike, but we understood each other perfectly. We shared everything—our dreams, our doubts. He was absolutely trustworthy. He could keep a secret like no one else. He was wonderful." Until that moment, she hadn't realized how much she'd been yearning to talk about her brother.

When they reached the residence hall, Laura said, "I have to get to work—put away Hemingway and start reading Cervantes. See you tomorrow, okay?"

"Yeah, tomorrow."

That night Ellie lay in bed reliving the day. *When Laura shared her dream of visiting Paris, it was an invitation for me to tell my truth. I did, and my story didn't put her off for even an instant.* "I have a friend," she whispered, then rolled over and pulled the blanket up to her chin. *I told her about Danny. For a little while, I remembered him alive.*

She thought about what Professor Levin had said. *"You're standing on the threshold of the future. It's going to be an exciting time."* For the first time since arriving at Hunter, Ellie believed those words.

"BRAVE NEW WORLD"

1992

Mary O'Neal was on her hands and knees planting bulbs among the Christmas ferns at the edge of the walk that led to her white clapboard house. She spent each Saturday and Sunday outside—deadheading, pruning, and planting. Yesterday, one of her colleagues at the library said, "I suppose all the gardening you do in your free time helps keep your mind off the loss of Jimmy and Danny."

She was completely off target, Mary thought, as she pushed a strand of blonde hair out of her eyes. *I do it to keep my mind on them.* She relived precious memories as she worked. After the death of her husband and son the previous fall, she'd cried her fill every night for weeks. But her grief had evolved. Now more than anything, she remembered them alive. Remembered the laughter that used to fill their home. Her husband had done what he loved, loved everything he did, and both of her children had inherited his joyful response to life.

She'd planted bulbs each autumn of her adult life. In garden beds. Along the path that led to the lake at her family's little summer house. Naturalized in open areas of the woods. Gardening in memory of Jimmy and Danny on this bright October morning was a comfort. Made her happy. But thoughts of her living child made her heart hurt. Time had brought Ellie, her eighteen-year-old daughter, no comfort, no peace. Unable to believe she would ever be happy again, she'd left for college a month ago, a somber vestige of the ebullient girl she'd been a year earlier. Mary had written her twice but hadn't received a reply. Ellie was nothing if not considerate, so the lack of response was worrisome. *And yet, what can I do beyond expressing my love? I can't go down to the city and hold her hand. She wouldn't want that, and it wouldn't be right. All I can do is honor her along with her brother and father. And wait.*

While she worked, she tried to imagine her lovely girl—so forlorn now—full of joy, as she would be again one day.

The mailman stopped on his way to the porch. "Maybe you should take a break from digging and read your mail. Looks like something from your daughter: E. O'Neal, New York City. It's got a big heart drawn after your name."

"Yes, I will do that." She tugged off her gloves and carried the letter to the porch. Leaned against a faded pillow on the wooden swing and opened the envelope.

September 28, 1992

Dear Mom,

Thank you for the letters you've written. You've probably been waiting for a reply, but I couldn't bring myself to write back. Sorry. My classes are phenomenal, but I hadn't made a single friend until two days ago, and I couldn't bear to put down in words how lonely I felt. Now that I have a friend, I'll introduce her. Her name is Laura. She's from the Bronx. When I told her about Dad and Danny, she jumped up and hugged me. A minute later she took me by the hand. We walked three blocks to a subway station and headed for Greenwich Village where she bought me my first ever cappuccino. She's spontaneous and emotional, and her energy absolutely blazes. She's wonderful. I sat across from her the day we met and remembered the words Shakespeare gave Miranda, "O brave new world. That has such people in't." I have a feeling Laura and I will be friends forever.

I'll write more when I have time. I love you, Mom.

Ellie

Mary sighed. *Ellie's not alone in that big city. She has an amazing friend. I know how that feels.* Twenty-five years ago, shortly after meeting Jimmy, she herself had exclaimed Miranda's words. *Have I ever told Ellie? I don't think so, but that line is bound to occur to a reader of* The Tempest *whose eyes open onto a beautiful life-changing being.*

My emotional state when I met Jimmy was different from Ellie's. She's suffering the loss of a father and brother she deeply loved, whose love enriched her life, whereas my whole life felt impoverished. No one had ever told me they loved me. I'd never said the words myself.

Mary eventually came to realize her family had been dysfunctional—a cold, controlling father, a submissive mother who didn't fully participate in life—but as a young woman, she had no word for the neediness she felt. At age twenty-one, when she left Minnesota for graduate school, she sensed she'd been happy early in her childhood, but intervening years had obscured her memories. Each time she reached for one, it disappeared. There was an empty place inside her, a painful mystery. She couldn't fill the space.

Mary had arrived in Ithaca in 1967. *The summer of love.* The notion fascinated her. She had traveled to the Finger Lakes of New York, not the romantic city of San Francisco where hippies wore flowers in their hair, but the university on a hill, a thousand miles from her Midwest home, thrilled her. Her first morning there, she joined an energetic throng climbing a grassy slope toward the center of campus. Guys dressed in khakis and oxford cloth shirts or in jeans and tie-dyed tees. Girls wearing A-line dresses and Capezio flats like her own, and others in gauze blouses and flowing skirts. She walked among them, yet separate. An observer. "I'm not in Minnesota anymore," she said softly as she walked back down the hill.

Half an hour later as she stood in line at the bank, musing on what this new life might hold, a young man, dressed in jeans and a faded chambray shirt with sleeves rolled to the elbow, tapped her on the shoulder. He had a mop of unruly black curls and sparkling blue eyes. "Do you have a pen I might borrow?" he said in an accent she couldn't identify. She knew people had lots of different dialects in New York. She liked his.

"I do." She handed it to him.

He laid his checkbook across his palm and filled out the deposit slip, then returned the pen. "Thank you. I'm Jimmy."

"You're welcome. My name is Mary."

His eyes sparkled. "And where are you from, Mary?"

"Minnesota."

He gave a kind of half nod and narrowed his eyes. "I've never met anyone from Minnesota. What's it like out there?"

"Oh, it's . . . well . . . rural. I'm from a small town."

"Like this one?"

"No, not really. Smaller. Even Northfield, where I did my undergraduate work, is only half the size of Ithaca. And my hometown has just over two thousand people. Where are you from?"

"Brooklyn."

"Oh. So the way you talk, that's a Brooklyn accent?"

"Ha. I guess so, Irish Brooklyn. And the way you talk, that's a Minnesota accent?"

She shrugged. "I guess it is."

They reached the front of the line, and he invited her out for a beer "or, whatever you like to drink." They settled on that evening, and she gave him her address.

Jimmy was a talker. That night, over his three beers and Mary's two coffees, he told her his life story. His father had died in the Dublin bombing of 1941 before he was born. When he was a year old, he and his older brother, Johnny, moved to Brooklyn with their mother. "Mam died when I was four. My brother was nineteen. He let me sleep in his bed for months after her death. He raised me. Shepherded me through elementary and high school. Sent me to college in Brooklyn. It's been a rocky journey—a lot of ups and downs—but by next summer I'll have my Master of Engineering degree. Johnny says I'm about to do the family proud."

Jimmy's story could have been sad, but it wasn't. He knew more about the father he'd never met and the mother he'd known for only four years than Mary knew about the parents she'd lived with until she was eighteen. His life seemed rich and full of love, the opposite of hers.

He listened as well as he talked. She told him what little she knew about her family, and she shared her feelings—the emptiness inside her and the mystery she couldn't explain. He said, "If you can put up with my long-winded way, together we'll fill that empty space. And when the mystery is too much for you to bear alone, I'll help you carry it. We'll work as a team."

Within two weeks, they were a couple. Quiet, studious Mary Johnson from Eldon, Minnesota, and gregarious Jimmy O'Neal, from Ireland by way of Brooklyn. One night, as they walked downhill after their drinks at the Chapter House, he sang "The Rose of Tralee," an Irish ballad. "My brother used to sing it. I never had a clear picture of the Mary in the song until the day we met at the bank. As soon as you said your name, she was real. She was you." He kissed her good night at her door and walked away singing "Here, There and Everywhere" as if the Beatles had written it for him and her. She listened through the upstairs hall window for a minute, then turned away and echoed Miranda's words. "O brave new world . . . "

In twenty-four years of marriage, she never solved the mystery of her past, but she had known deep happiness, had heard the words "I love you" and said them herself, thousands of times. Her husband and their son and daughter had filled the empty space inside her.

Mary reread the last line of her daughter's letter, "I have a feeling Laura and I will be friends forever." The words rang off the page. The facts of Ellie's life hadn't changed, but her outlook had. *She'll still have to bear the sorrow, but she has hope for the future. I'm going to commemorate this day.* She picked up the trowel and basket of bulbs and walked between clouds of white anemones and stands of fiery crocosmias toward a lilac bush in the southeast corner of the yard. At its base, between two hostas, she dug a hole just the size for five daffodils and patted dark soil over the golden brown bulbs. They would send out roots and lie in wait through the winter until April, when yellow blooms would spring up in celebration of her daughter's new world.

BEING BROTHERS

1995

David Campbell picked up his mail, stepped onto the elevator, and loosened his tie. As he rode up to the first floor, he casually flipped through various bills and flyers. It wasn't until he stood in his kitchen prioritizing them that he noticed the yellow envelope with a U.S. postmark and his mother's exuberant, sweeping handwriting. He opened a beer and sat down to read her letter.

Tompkins County, NY

May 10, 1995

Dear David,

We've finally finished the Serrano ham you sent for Easter. We served it for dinners, lunches, and breakfasts. It lasted almost a month, and every slice was delicious. Thank you for sharing that Spanish treat.

I have a favor to ask. You know that Andrew will be finishing his postgraduate programme in London this year. And he's fallen in love. Without meaning to, he left a string of broken hearts on his search for the right girl, but he finally found her. He went all the way to England and met someone from here in the Finger Lakes who's studying at King's College. She's a literature student who happens to have a passion for a Spanish novelist named Galdós, and Andrew wants to surprise her with a visit to Madrid before they head back home. Could you invite them and put them up, maybe give them an introduction to the city? I know Andrew would appreciate an invitation.

Ellie, the girl he loves, sounds delightful. He'll be bringing her here to meet your dad and me at the end of June. You'll meet her before we do. You can share your brother's happiness with him.

Take care, David.

Love, Mom

David would've preferred email, but he decided to respond to his mother in kind. He jotted a quick note.

Madrid, Spain

May 18, 1995

Mom-

Yeah, I've got Andrew's phone number. I'll be glad to give him a call. I can congratulate him on being the first Campbell son to fall in love, for besting me at something for once in his life. Just kidding. I'll be totally gracious. I look forward to having him here.

Love to you and Dad,

David

Andrew and Ellie showed up at David's apartment at noon on a scorching June day. Despite having travelled four hours by train from London, nineteen on the ferry from Plymouth, and five more on a bus from Santander, they looked remarkably well groomed and fresh. David gripped Andrew's hand and patted his back. "Welcome, bro."

A flush of pleasure colored Andrew's face. "This is Ellie." She reached out and hugged David. There were tears in her eyes.

"Come on in and sit down. I thought you'd be sweaty and disheveled after your trip. I was going to offer you an immediate shower, but neither of you appears to need one."

"That's Ellie's doing," Andrew said. "She packed clean clothes for each of us at the top of her backpack. She wanted to make a good impression. We washed up and changed at the bus station twenty minutes ago."

Ellie pushed back a stray blonde curl and wiped a tear from her cheek. "This duffle is full of dirty shirts and underwear and two wet towels. No gift for our host." She smiled in apology. "Just soiled laundry."

"Okay, then," David said. "What first? Coffee? A nap? Your choice."

Andrew turned to Ellie with the yearning look of a guy who'd spent the last day and a half on public transportation with a girl he was wild about. What he wanted was to be alone with her. "We may look fresh, but we could both use a shower, then a rest before coffee. Does that sound good, Ellie?"

"It sounds great to me. And then we'll go to the Puerta del Sol." She looked expectantly from Andrew to David.

"A woman with an agenda. I like that," David said. He showed them to their room and closed the door. *Oh Andrew,* he thought, *you lucky guy.*

Half an hour later the two guests emerged laughing. "I'm going to relax and unwind for a while," Andrew said, "but Ellie really does want to go straight to the Puerta del Sol. Is that feasible?"

"Well, maybe." David looked at Ellie. "Do you speak Spanish?"

"A little. Actually, I only read it, but I think I can get by."

He tried to suppress a smile. "That might work. Are you sure you don't want to wait and go with Andrew?"

"He doesn't know a word of Spanish, and he's not interested in the city the way I am. How far is it? Can I walk?"

"About half an hour on foot. Are you a good walker?"

"I'm an excellent walker, and I've dreamed of visiting the center of Madrid for two years. I spent my freshman year of college reading *Fortunata y Jacinta* aloud with my friend Laura. I want to walk where the characters lived."

"Andrew, how do you feel about it? Are you comfortable with Ellie walking across a strange city alone?"

"Hey, it's her choice. She's been dying to do this since the day we decided to visit you. It's not dangerous, is it?"

David shrugged and looked at Ellie. "No, not dangerous. Maybe a little challenging."

"Well, I don't mind a challenge," she said. "Do you have a map?"

He took one from a drawer and handed it to her. She studied it for a minute. "So we're here, and here's where I'm going. It looks pretty straightforward except for these little streets in the center. When I get there, I'll wander from one place to another. I'll be back in a few hours." She kissed each of them and walked out the door.

"Wow, does she always take control like that?" David asked. "I think you may be punching above your weight. She's like Mom."

"Actually, she's not. She has Mom's energy, but she's fragile. She's had some sad years. You saw the tears in her eyes when she hugged you. She lost her brother when she was seventeen, and she's got this romantic notion of brotherhood that doesn't really fit the Campbell pattern. That's what she is—romantic. Going to the Puerta del Sol by herself will be a romantic adventure."

"It'll definitely be an adventure. A lovely young blue-eyed blonde, speaking schoolgirl Spanish in the center of Madrid. I'd probably be jealous, more protective than you are."

"Oh, I'm not the jealous kind. And Ellie doesn't need protection. She exudes innocence but always manages to take care of herself. She's special. Battered but not beaten—hopeful. You're gonna love her."

"I'm sure I will. Come on. Let's grab a beer. There's a cafe on the plaza a couple of minutes from here. You can tell me how you met while we walk." They took the elevator down and stepped out onto the narrow tree-lined street.

◆

"God, it was my lucky day," Andrew said, "the second Saturday in September. I had a rare weekend off. I was sitting on the steps of Somerset House overlooking the Thames. An American voice floated across the terrace, and I turned and saw this appealing girl. I called out, 'What's a teenage girl from the Finger Lakes doing in London?' I knew there was no way in hell she was from there; I just wanted to get her attention. I thought she'd say, 'What are the Finger Lakes?' But she turned to me in a wide-open way and said, 'I'm not a teenager, but that is where I'm from. How could you tell?' I made up something about being good with voices. That's how we met."

"Hmm, interesting pickup line. I guess the rest of the day went well."

"Yeah, it did. We walked through central London laughing, until something I said changed the tone. She told me about her dad and brother dying three years earlier. She was really attached to her brother. I wonder sometimes what she'd be like if she hadn't lost him."

"Certainly different, but losing him—both of them—made her the person she is, the person you love."

"Yeah, you're probably right," Andrew said, "but I wonder."

They crossed the plaza and took a table in the shade. Andrew watched and listened as his brother nodded to a server and began an animated exchange. *God, he's only lived here a year, and he's completely confident, speaking Spanish like a native.* David had always been smooth and self-assured. Someone once described him as too big for their little Finger Lakes world. That's how Andrew had seen him, too—larger than life, full of drive and wise-ass comments.

He remembered their mom telling a friend, *"You've heard of speed reading. Well, David's a speed thinker."*

She meant it as a compliment, but Andrew hadn't been sure. *I thought he probably missed out on a lot of important stuff by thinking so fast. I was almost seventeen before I appreciated him. God, what a summer that was.* "You remember the year I met Jessie Thorne?"

David threw his head back. "O-oh yeah."

"I never thanked you for your—what should I call it—your tact? Most of all, for not letting on to Mom and Dad that I was sleeping with her."

"Ha, as if anyone needed to tell them. Your surging testosterone filled the house. The rest of us had to go outside to breathe."

"So they knew? You think they approved?"

"I don't know if they approved, but what were they going to say to their full-grown son who was working almost sixty hours a week on the farm?" He lifted his beer in a glib toast. "They were probably relieved that their little nature lover was finally showing interest in a human life form."

Andrew laughed. He and his cool, accomplished older brother were sitting together, adults, equals. *And I'm the one in love with the most wonderful woman in the world. Who'd have thought?*

Three hours later, David buzzed Ellie up, and he and Andrew listened to her breathless account of the afternoon. "I walked from the Puerta del Sol to the Plaza de Santa Cruz and the Plaza Mayor and down every little street. A lawyer from Galicia helped me with my Spanish. He showed me how to order tapas—there's an art to it—and walked with me to the house where Galdós lived when he moved to Madrid. On my way back here, I stopped at his monument in Retiro Park." She beamed. "I had a fabulous afternoon. Thank you, Andrew, for bringing me here. Thank you, David, for inviting us. Thank you both so much."

"You walked for three hours," Andrew said, "and I'm the one who's yawning. I need a nap. Don't you?"

"I'm too excited now. I'll sleep later."

When Andrew left the room, David stayed behind watching Ellie. She pulled a battered paperback from her pack and curled up on the sofa. Head bowed over the book, she flipped back and forth as she read—underlining passages, writing notes. When she glanced up and noticed David staring, she blushed. "I always write a lot in my books. I dog-ear the pages too. It's for when I reread. I reread everything I love. Do you read fiction?"

"Not so much. I doubt that Andrew does either."

"No, mostly science and philosophy. We did read *Hamlet* together though." She smiled. "He called the sweet Danish prince an Epicurean. I read him Shakespeare and he taught me squash. He said a wise woman once told him that everyone should know how to play at least one ball-game." She stopped and looked out the window over David's head. "You guys are lucky to have each other. To have time to be brothers together. My brother died when he was fourteen." She paused again. "Andrew understands death. Did you know that? He's trying to help me come to terms with it."

David knew nothing about Andrew's insights on death. "Yeah, that's good," he said. When Ellie went back to her reading, he continued to watch her leaning against the arm of the sofa, knees pulled up like a child, balancing her book, scribbling away. She sat quietly absorbed as if she were alone in the room, but he knew if he engaged her, she'd stop reading and respond with enthusiasm. *She's enchanting, and she's in love with my brother.*

He walked into the kitchen. *My little brother's all grown up,* he thought as he washed and dried his breakfast dishes. He remembered Andrew as a quiet, thoughtful child, intent on observing the woods and fields. *I never paid much attention to him until the year he was sixteen. I saw his work ethic that summer. Got a glimpse of the man he might become. Now he's on his way to Columbia to work on a doctorate. He's found the woman of his dreams.* David chuckled. *Maybe he has one-upped me.*

Twenty-eight hours of travel and a three-hour walk through Madrid finally caught up with Ellie. She stretched her legs the full length of the sofa and sighed. "I've had a beautiful day."

She lay asleep hugging her dog-eared book when Andrew and David left to buy sandwiches at a deli and was still out when they returned. The clatter of plates and glasses, the repeated thud of the refrigerator door, didn't rouse her. Sounds that floated up from the street when they opened the French doors had no effect. She didn't stir.

———◆———

An hour later Ellie awoke to voices on the balcony. Andrew and David, challenging each other. Talking over one another. Laughter, then silence followed by raised voices and more laughter. She picked up the book that had slipped onto the floor, but she didn't read. Just lay still and listened. They weren't tender with each other like she and her brother had been. *They're playing a verbal squash game,* she thought. *Competing. Calling faults on each other. But it's crossfire without a shred of anger. It's a way of caring. They're being brothers together.*

"MOTHER
NATURE'S SON"

2006

Four-year-old Danny Campbell, lean and wiry, with hair the color of a new penny and startlingly blue eyes, could scarcely contain his enthusiasm. He leaned from his booster seat toward the front of the car so his father, Andrew, could hear every word. "I have something important to show you. Last Monday, Grandma and Grandpa let me explore by myself, and I discovered a new bird. I don't know its name, so today we'll search for it together and you can tell me." He stopped to catch his breath. "Let's walk in the woods before we go in the house, okay?"

"Yep, that's what we'll do," Andrew said, as he pulled to a stop on the gravel path that led to his parents' Finger Lakes farmhouse and got out of the car. "You be the leader." The mixed woodland—a leafy canopy of maples and beeches, an understory of shrubs and saplings, and a floor of ferns and tangled vines—beckoned. Andrew loved it all, the bright open patches and the dark alcoves where the summer sun never reached. The thicket was his heart's home.

He watched his son, trudging purposefully through the underbrush. *Sharing the wonder of nature with him, allowing him space to observe its constancy and its fluctuation, is the most important thing I do.* The two of them had started daily outdoor adventures—watching squirrels, birds, and ants in their Brooklyn neighborhood—before Danny could walk. The rules for exploring nature that he laid out for his son were ones he followed himself. "Watch the plants and animals. Never bother them. And always ask questions."

The bond they forged was lively and tranquil and flexible enough to grow with Danny. After two days of preschool, the three-year-old had looked over at Andrew as they crawled on hands and knees through their tiny city garden. "You know, Dad, I'm a school boy now. I have a best friend. His name is Zack. But don't worry. I'll always be your friend."

Danny grabbed Andrew's hand and yanked him into the present. "Look, Dad." He pointed up at a low branch in a sugar maple. "See the little orange and black bird hopping between the leaves? It's the one I discovered. The one whose name I want to know."

Andrew looked up and followed the flashing trajectory of the bird. "It's an American Redstart."

"Wow, American Redstart," Danny repeated with satisfaction. "I bet you know the name of every bird."

"No, I don't, but I do know that one." The bird's darting flight accompanied by Danny's *wow* carried him back to the year he turned seven. To the day he first encountered the tiny warbler.

❖

On that summer day, Andrew had gone up to his room after breakfast and pulled on a pair of threadbare jeans and a soft, faded tee shirt. *I like being this age,* he thought. *I'm old enough to choose my own clothes and make my own plans.* School had been out for almost a month. He could do what he wanted all day with no teacher to interrupt his thoughts. As he walked down the stairs that led to the kitchen, he mused, *Which is the real world? The one we can see with a magnifying glass or the one we see without it?* He liked the back stairs. They were a private place to think because no one else in the family used them. The steps were too narrow for big feet, for people in a hurry. *Everyone in this family is big and busy. Everyone but me.*

His mother, Jane, was talking to his older brother at the kitchen table. "It might be fun for Andrew to go with you today."

"He has no interest whatsoever in baseball." David's deep voice belied his eleven years. "He spends his days looking at life through that magnifying glass Dad gave him last fall. You and Dad need to face the truth, Mom. He's bizarre."

"Not bizarre. Andrew is curious in every sense of the word. Dad thinks we've got ourselves a family philosopher. You never know what ideas he'll come up with. He might like to go to the game with you. Ask him. If he wants to, we could pick up Finn on the way into town."

"Oh, Mom, I'm not really up for a lecture on the Knights of the Round Table from a six-year-old. Finn's even weirder than-"

The room went silent as Andrew jumped down the last step. He'd heard the whole conversation. David said he was bizarre. He thought that might mean he wasn't good at sports. But his mom said he was curious. He knew what that meant. *I am curious; that's a good thing.* "Mom, guess what? I've been looking at the stairway through my magnifying glass. The wood looks smooth, but it's actually covered with jaggedy grooves that you can't see with the naked eye. So I'm wondering if you think-"

David interrupted, "Hey, Andrew, Mom's going to drop me off in town for a baseball game. You want to go? You could call Finn, and we could take him along."

"Nah, Finn can't come. He's going to a kids' class about the legend of King Arthur." Andrew had mixed feelings about the invitation. He wasn't good at playing baseball, and he didn't like to watch it.

He thought David, and even Mom and Dad, might be proud of him if he managed to sit through a whole ball game, but he knew he wouldn't be able to. They always lasted too long. He'd get bored and end up crawling under the bleachers searching through thrown away scraps for valuable stuff, and David would get ticked off. He wouldn't yell, but he'd act embarrassed. "I don't think so." Andrew needed an excuse, something important to do at home. "I have to explore the thicket today," he said.

David muttered. "He *has to* explore the thicket?"

Jane ignored him and smiled at Andrew. "That sounds like an adventure. Shall I pack you a lunch?"

"Nope, I'll make myself a sandwich." When his mom and David took off in the car, Andrew spread peanut butter on one slice of whole wheat bread and honey on another. He squashed them together, filled a thermos with milk, grabbed an apple from a bowl on the counter, and put everything in a knapsack. He hung his dad's binoculars around his neck, put the magnifying glass in his jeans pocket, and headed for the woods.

Saying I had to explore the thicket was a lie. He'd been planning to wander around in the house and outside—not doing anything—but his mom was right. Exploring it would be an adventure. He'd use the binoculars for far away and the magnifying glass for close up. He leaned the knapsack against a beech tree at the edge of the woods and searched the leafy branches above with the binoculars. He tried to focus on a bright orange and black bird perched on a branch over his head, but it moved so fast the binoculars were of no use. He let them hang around his neck as he watched, but when the bird flew into the underbrush and Andrew got down on his hands and knees for a closer look, they were in the way. He took them off and laid them and the magnifying glass on top of the knapsack.

The bird would be quiet for a second, then chirp out a sharp vibrating sound. It hopped quick as a wink from one spot to another, among the plants on the ground and from branch to branch above. Andrew watched transfixed, absolutely still, as the bird flashed its wings and fanned its tail. It would fly at insects, attack and catch them in mid-air. He didn't care what David thought. *Watching this bird is way better than sitting at a ball game.*

He followed its every move until his dad drove up the path that bordered the woods and rolled down the window of the pickup. "Andrew, do you want to come with me to inspect the crops we'll be picking for tomorrow's market? You can be my official taster."

"Sure, but I may eat quite a lot. I skipped my lunch. I've been busy."

"You eat as much as you want. We've got plenty. But it's not like you to go without lunch. What's kept you so busy?"

"Come on. I'll show you. I've been watching a bird for ages." His dad stepped out of the truck and Andrew took him by the hand. He pointed to the active little orange and black bird. "It's an amazing bug catcher. It's taking food to a bird up in that nest."

"You're right, son. He's an American Redstart, quite an acrobatic little fellow. The bird in the nest is a female incubating a clutch of eggs, and he's feeding her while she keeps them warm."

Andrew whispered, "Wow. American Redstarts. A father and a mother. And pretty soon there'll be babies."

"Right. Now let's go sample some peas and strawberries."

The time he spent exploring that day was the beginning of a lifelong quest for Andrew. Over the years, he examined the fabric of life in the patch of woods. Studied organisms interacting with their environment and detected a pattern—intricate and grand—within the apparent disarray. Watched rivals—flora as well as fauna—compete for territory. Learned relationships between prey and predators, parents and offspring, mated pairs. As he observed the natural order, he discovered where he belonged in the world. The woods offered him the gift of himself. More than once his brother had called him "Mother Nature's Son." David likely meant it as a gibe, but Andrew took it as a compliment.

The circumstances of his life evolved and wherever he was, he carried the woods within. They never abandoned him. Today he was back where he started, sharing their gift with his son.

Danny gave Andrew's hand another tug, jerked him out of his reverie. "Come on, Dad. Let's sit here under this tree, as quiet as anything, and watch for a while." They sat on the ground together and breathed in the wonder of the world. Father and son passed ten full minutes in silence, observing the teeming activity that surrounded them. Pointing out bright birds, a spider spinning a silver web, brown beetles and green leafhoppers. At last Danny whispered, "Can we talk now?"

"Sure, what do you want to say?"

"Only one thing."

"Okay, go for it."

Sunlight slipped between the leaves of a sugar maple and dappled the little boy's face. "I'm having a wonderful childhood."

ORDINARY PEOPLE

2007

Mandy and Ethan sat in their Manhattan dining room reading their preferred sections of *The New York Times,* Obituaries and International. The rest of the paper lay fanned across the table, awaiting leisurely perusal. With their six-year-old, Mary, not expected home from a sleepover until noon, the two of them luxuriated in the relaxed pace of a purely adult morning.

Reading the paper at Sunday breakfast was a tradition. In 1998, when they moved in together, Ethan had been baffled by the section Mandy liked to read. Obituaries, not the ones of famous people, the paid ones. "Why do you want to read about the deaths of people no one's ever heard of?"

She'd rejoined, "Why do you want to read novels about the lives of imaginary people?"

"You can't compare obituaries to literature."

"I can." Mandy was an endodontist. She read nonfiction, not novels. "This is life and death," she said, "of real people." She'd scan the page and choose the stories she wanted to read aloud—of a young woman who'd left behind a husband and children or a rabbi eulogized by a dozen different congregants. "We're all connected. As one of your poets said, 'No man is an island.' "

With typical fervor, she announced her first choice of the day. "Here's one. Don't tell me this true story about an ordinary family isn't as worthy of reflection as any piece of fiction." She began reading aloud, "Andrew Campbell, a professor of biochemistry at Columbia, and his five-year-old son, Danny, died at University Hospital in Newark from injuries sustained in an auto accident on October 10, 2007, leaving behind . . . oh my god-"

"Yeah, what a tragedy for a wife—to lose her husband and her son."

"Ethan, I think you may know the wife."

"I doubt it. I don't know many scientists. I've never even met a biochemist."

"Not the husband. I said you may know his wife. You told me about her the year we met. Ellinor. That's the wife's name. Her maiden name was O'Neal. Wasn't that your girlfriend from the Finger Lakes?"

"Ellie O'Neal, yes, but she was never called Ellinor. Does it say where they're from?"

"Brooklyn, but he went to school in Ithaca. He's a couple of years older than you. I'm sure it's her. It must be. Oh god, I'm so sorry."

"Don't jump to conclusions." He reached for the paper. "Let me see it." He read the short paragraph about the man. Thirty-five years old. High school in Ithaca. Studied at MIT, King's College in London, and Columbia. Of course, there was no information about his wife—only her name—Ellinor Campbell, née O'Neal. *It can't be Ellie,* he thought. *Someone, one of her parents or a teacher, would've called her Ellinor at one time or another.* But there was the maiden name and the Finger Lakes connection. And the son's name, Danny, was her brother's name. Too many coincidences. He took a quick breath. "It is Ellie. And she wasn't just any girlfriend. She was the first girl I loved. We met my sophomore year of high school. I wrote a piece about her for an undergrad composition course. I don't think I ever showed it to you."

"You didn't. If you saved it, I'd like to hear it."

"I'm sure it's in a folder." He opened his laptop and pulled up the Word document. "Here it is 'Love Lost.' God, it's five pages long, and I have no idea of the quality of my writing at the time. Sure you're up for listening?"

"It's Sunday morning. Mary's at the Greens'. We just read an obituary of a person you have a connection to. I've got nothing better to do than listen." She poured them each another cup of coffee. Ethan started reading.

Love Lost

My dad thought the rarified atmosphere we lived in—Westchester County and private schools and too much money—wasn't good for my sister and me. Somehow he worked out an offbeat deal with my school. I'd spend my sophomore and junior year of high school in the little Finger Lakes town he'd visited in summers as a kid. He thought of it as a clever twist on study abroad. After two years among down-to-earth people in the Finger Lakes, I'd return to prep school ready for my senior year and life.

My mother didn't want to move. She stalled so long that we didn't arrive in Cremona until after the holidays. I started school there in January of 1990. I'd actually been looking forward to living in a small town. Thought it might be a cool adventure. The reality was nothing like what I'd imagined. Dad had filled my head with stories of friendly people who were hard working and full of common sense. I thought kids would welcome me, teach me to—I don't know—chop wood, shovel snow. I guess they did do those things, but they weren't interested in teaching me. I had expected they'd want to know about city life, but they couldn't have cared less. I was a curiosity. They stared. Whispered. Mimicked the way I talked.

Dad told me to buck up, go out for basketball, invite kids over to the house. I did. It worked, sort of. I got to play junior varsity ball and was invited to a few parties. Life was okay. Not great, but okay. The best part of each school day was literature class. The teacher—Mrs. Bradford was her name—was a thoughtful woman, about thirty years old. She taught us Red Badge of Courage. Really taught it. Encouraged us to think, to talk. And she listened like no adult I'd ever known.

That's where I met Ellie. She was, hands down, the brightest kid in the class, but instead of flaunting her intellect with pretentious answers, she asked questions that made the rest of us smarter.

I asked Amy, who seemed to be her best friend, why Ellie never showed up at parties. "Ah, she doesn't like 'em. Nothing against the people who throw them, but parties aren't her thing."

Although she'd lived in Cremona her whole life, Ellie didn't fit in any better than I did. But she didn't care. Self contained, with a smile that radiated contentment, she quietly marched to the beat of her own drum. Her style—a kind of wholesome version of grunge—set her apart from every other girl in school, and it fascinated me. Her long blonde hair always seemed tangled by the wind. Every day that winter she wore an oversized long-sleeved plaid flannel shirt knotted at the waist over a white tee, with black leggings and Converse sneakers. When it started to get warm, she exchanged the flannel shirts for chambray, and by the middle of May she ditched the shirts and leggings. Wore a long tee, belted with a macramé sash, as a dress, and tan suede Birkenstocks instead of sneakers.

On the last day of school, I followed her out of our classroom and invited her to hang out sometimes during the summer. Maybe play tennis or sail. She seemed disappointed, said she'd never played tennis in her life. "I wouldn't be much of a partner, and I'm a really lame sailor." Then her face brightened. "But I have an idea. I can tell you like literature—as much as I do. Would you like to read together?"

That's how it started. "You go first," she said the day we met by the lake to read. I'd chosen *Catcher in the Rye*. It was kind of a guy's book. I had last-minute doubts about reading it aloud, but when I paused at the end of each chapter, Ellie would wave me on. It wasn't until I'd read almost fifty pages that she indicated I could stop. She said, "Holden has a good heart. I understand why you feel the way you do about him." I doubted that she understood my feelings about him. I wasn't even sure I did. But I was glad she liked the book.

She chose *Romeo and Juliet*. I'd read the play. I didn't like it. But as she read, I fell in love with Juliet. She was no longer some anonymous fourteenth century girl. She was intelligent and compassionate, as alive as Ellie. Day after day, we walked along the lake and analyzed Romeo's and Juliet's and Holden Caulfield's teenage angst, and we fell in love. Innocent, but with a sexy pulse running through it.

The O'Neals were great—industrious and fun-loving—the kind of ordinary people my father would have wanted me to meet, if he'd been able to imagine them. Ellie's dad was an engineer who loved boats and could play and sing every 60s-era song. Her mom was a librarian. Had actually read *Catcher in the Rye*. Her brother, Danny, was an easygoing kid, a super talented sailor. I think I fell in love with her family as much as I did with Ellie.

They spent summers in a one-room cottage by the lake. It was rustic, but pristine, with handsewn quilts and handbuilt furniture. A late twentieth century take on Arts and Crafts. They all slept on the same porch. It blew me away. "You all sleep together?" I asked her one afternoon. "When do your mom and dad have . . . privacy?"

She echoed me, "Privacy?" then waited a beat. "On Saturdays, Dad and Mom drive to our house in town to do laundry. I guess that's when. The summer I was twelve, I told Mom I'd take over the task. She thanked me but didn't accept my offer. Told me she and Dad needed some time alone together." Ellie laughed and rolled her eyes. "It took me all year to put one and one together, to figure out why they might want privacy."

I started to feel like part of the O'Neal family. I think my dad was happy for me, but my mother disapproved. Ellie, my bright, beautiful girlfriend, had lunch at our house one day. Afterwards, Mom said, "The girl would be quite attractive if she combed her hair and dressed appropriately." I actually despised my mother at that moment.

I should've guessed what was about to happen, but I didn't. At the beginning of August, Dad said, "Ethan, your mother and I have been thinking that maybe you should go back to boarding school next year."

I was incensed. I didn't believe he thought that. I shouted at him, "It's Mom, isn't it? She can't stand my being with a girl who's not impressed by our house and our money. A sixteen-year-old who's already had more thoughts than Mom's had in forty years."

My parents laid out their plan. They'd stay in the house they had leased in Cremona throughout the coming school year, but my sister and I'd return to boarding school and meet them for holidays at our grand-parents' home in Florida.

I cried when I told Ellie. She stared fixedly at some spot in the distance. "They want to keep you away from me, don't they?"

"Not Dad, but maybe my mom." Her face went from stony to soft. She laid her head on my shoulder and sobbed.

We vowed to stay together, but by the end of the month I capitu-lated. "It's not going to work," I told her. "They're in control." The after-noon we met to say goodbye was sunny, but cold for August, with wind off the lake whipping Ellie's hair into a golden cloud. I brushed it out of her eyes, and ran my fingers down her cheek, wishing for a miraculous intervention that never came. Finally I said, "I love you," and turned and walked away. I never saw her again.

I was miserable for the entire school year. I missed Ellie and hated myself for not being strong enough to defend her. For failing to stand up to my parents. I didn't speak to them for nine months.

The next summer Dad arranged for me to talk to a therapist. I forgave myself and my dad, even my mother. The counselor thought it might be good for me to write Ellie. I knew he was wrong. What would I say after all that time? "Sorry, Ellie, for walking away like that and ignoring you for a whole year." I told him I couldn't do it. I never contacted her.

Ethan closed the document and shook his head. "God, I just walked away. I wish . . . I wish . . . ." He couldn't go on. He wasn't sure what he wished.

"You could contact her now," Mandy said softly. "It's easy to find people these days—Google, LinkedIn."

He googled Ellinor O. Campbell. Found the independent publishing house she worked for and read her bio. *BA in Literatures and Languages, Hunter College; MA in English and American Literature, NYU . . . especially loves modern work that creatively reimagines classic literature.* He remembered how Ellie had laughed with glee upon discovering that Holden Caulfield admired Romeo's friend Mercutio. No doubt, Ellinor O. Campbell was the girl he fell in love with the summer he was sixteen.

He wrote and rewrote an email. Deleted it and started again. "Ellie, I'm so sorry for your loss . . . ." He deleted it one last time. Even if he were to get the sentiment right, it wasn't a proper way to connect after such a tragedy. And it wasn't the right time. *Someday,* he thought. *Maybe someday.*

FAMILY TIES

2007

Images of the second Wednesday in October played continuously in Jane Campbell's head. Sun shining on her grandson's red-gold hair. His voice, sweet and clear, as he called to her husband, Mark, from his booster seat. *"Grandpa, don't forget to bring the humongous pumpkin I picked for you when you come down to our house. I'll help you cut it."*

She remembered the warmth of her son Andrew's hand through the open window of the car as he said goodbye. *"I love you guys. We'll see you in three weeks."* Jane and Mark watched as he and Danny drove down the gravel path and away from the farm—for the last time. That afternoon, less than an hour from their Brooklyn home, a jackknifing semi collided with their Jetta. By six thirty, Andrew and Danny were gone. Life—chock-full of day-to-day work and play, rich with love and plans for the future—had been stopped short for them and transformed for the people who loved them.

"How will we live without them?" she repeated time and again to Mark. Tears would fill his eyes and he'd take her hand. He couldn't speak.

When Jane asked that question of Andrew's wife, Ellie, she didn't reply. She had awakened from sedation the day after the accident, crying, "No, no, no." But since that day there had been no tears. No flicker in her eyes. She had locked the pain deep inside.

The agony of the weeks that followed was beyond anything Jane could have imagined. The stab of her own pain was exacerbated by her empathy for Ellie. By the fear that their beloved daughter-in-law would not survive the loss of her husband and son.

Jane was a scientist, a practical woman who believed in availing herself of what modern psychotherapy had to offer. She talked and cried at weekly sessions. And she repeated the question. "How will we live without them? I need an answer."

"I can't give you one," her therapist said. "Simply live each moment; you'll find your answer in the living."

"I want to speak on my daughter-in-law's behalf. I want to help her find an answer as well."

"You can't live for her. She must do that for herself."

"But she's not living. She's moved back into her house in Brooklyn. Even returned to her old job. I called the head of the publishing house where she works to get his take on her emotional state. He said, 'Ellie's editing is stellar. She's fine as long as no one tries to engage her in personal conversation.' "

Jane gasped and shook her head. "Those words didn't diminish my concern. Ellie walks about in a semi-stupor. She wakes, goes to work, returns home, sleeps. I'm afraid she considers me some well-meaning woman who stops by and serves her food she doesn't want to eat. How will she discover her answer if she can't participate in her own life? It's a Catch-22."

"You've told me about her past—the loss of her father and younger brother in a fire when she was seventeen, then the death of her mother. Now she's confronting another violent, double loss. She's protecting herself from feelings she can't deal with."

"I know. I know. And that's why she, burdened by a life so fraught with pain, should be seeing someone. But she refuses. The only will she exhibits is a steadfast denial of her need for therapy."

"So, she has a will. That should encourage you. Watch her closely. One day you'll hear a sob, perhaps detect a smile, and you'll know she's making progress. Accept the way she's living and love her while you live your own life. That's the best thing you can do for her."

And Jane, compliant patient that she was, did exactly that. It was no chore to love Ellie. She spent every Saturday and Sunday in Brooklyn with her. They'd go to the market, walk to the botanic garden, do laundry together. She made no comment on Ellie's questionable life choices—the uneaten meals, the nights spent fully clothed on a sofa, the avoidance of mirrors—she just loved her.

At Mark and Jane's invitation, Ellie visited them on the farm every few weeks. She responded dutifully to their simple questions, stiffly to their touch. Displayed no emotion. *Blunted affect* is what the therapist called it. Jane wanted to rock her and cry with her, but she restrained herself. *I'll give her all the time she needs.*

One day in May, she and Mark stood beside Ellie as she looked through the upstairs hall window toward the edge of the woods. "That was Andrew's favorite spot." Her voice was tender. "He told me he discovered his place in the world while he examined life in the thicket. He and Danny explored it together every time we came up here."

Alert to the faintest expression of emotion, Mark said, "Oh yes, he loved those woods. Made me promise I'd never clear out the underbrush." Ellie turned away from the window without response. He touched her shoulder and waited a moment. Her desperate silence filled the room. Sharing thoughts about Andrew and Danny had depleted her, but he and Jane were encouraged. She had remembered life before the deaths, and spoken of it.

A month later Ellie made another foray into the past. Her question was tentative. "Do you remember . . . Laura?"

"Of course," Jane replied. "She's your soul sister."

The flicker of happiness that crossed Ellie's face was quickly replaced by a look of alarm. "She wasn't here last fall. I never called. She doesn't know."

Jane patted Ellie's arm. "She does know. I called her. She'd love to hear from you."

"Is she still living in Egypt?"

"Yes. She'll be there for another six months. I have her number."

The next morning at eight o'clock, Ellie made the call. Her first words were stilted. "Laura, this is your friend . . . Ellie." And the ones that followed were sparse. "Yes . . . I know . . . yes . . . so do I," and finally, "I love you too." She hung up and turned to Jane. "Laura cried and cried. She misses me and Andrew and Danny. She loves us all." Ellie paused. "And I know you and Mark do. I-" She didn't finish the sentence.

Jane closed her eyes and breathed a prayer of thanks. *She feels loved.*

She still adamantly refused to see a psychologist. "I'm out in the world working. I have you and Mark, and now Laura. I won't talk to a professional. I don't need one." So Jane waited. Loved her and waited.

At the beginning of September—almost a year after the accident—Ellie called Jane. Her voice was hoarse, but it glistened with hope. "I just listened to Joan Baez singing 'Danny Boy.' I sat in my kitchen and cried out loud about Andrew and Danny for an hour. Something inside me broke free. I want to live, but I don't know how to start."

"You've already started."

Three weeks later, Ellie drove to the farm and shared her plan. "I'm closing up our house and flying to England next week. I couldn't participate when you celebrated Andrew's and Danny's lives a year ago. Now I'm going to retrace the steps Andrew and I took in London the year we met—the beginning of the relationship that brought us all Danny. I'm going to live each moment in honor of the two of them, of what we shared."

She hugged Mark and Jane as they walked to her car. "Thank you for loving me, for being my parents." Tears streamed down her cheeks. "Here I go. Wish me luck."

Two days into her stay in London, Ellie sent a text that started a thread.

Dear Jane and Mark - I visited the Natural History Museum in honor of Andrew yesterday. I could sense Danny skipping along beside me, whooping with joy as he encountered those amazing dinosaurs. Love, Ellie.

My dear Ellie - I whooped with joy the first time I saw them. And I was twenty-four. Love, Mark

M and J - By the way, I called myself a widow yesterday. It made me cry to say it, but it's an important step, don't you think? Ellie

Absolutely, Ellie. Bravo! Jane

Jane and Mark - I have a new friend, Will. He's a professor of public policy and human rights here in London, but he grew up on a farm in Yorkshire. He loves Shakespeare like I do, and he plays squash like Andrew did. He lets me cry and makes me smile. He's walking me back to the world of the living. Love, E

Ellie - Shakespeare lover, squash player, and a farm background? Sounds like the right man to accompany you on that journey. We're happy for you. Love, Mark

Jane and Mark - You'll be pleased to know I'm taking your advice—seeing a therapist. Will wore me down with a list of irrefutable talking points. It's a good thing. Love, Ellie

Yes, Ellie - A very good thing. Love, Jane.

J and M - I finally invited Will to my flat. Showed him my photos of Andrew and Danny. Now he's seen them. He knows their faces. Love, E

My dear Ellie - Sharing those photos—connecting your past with someone in your present—is something to celebrate. Jane

The thread continued until Ellie announced she was flying home. At JFK, Laura ran to her with open arms and carried her back to Brooklyn. They wrapped each other in the security of unreserved friendship until the day

Laura said, "Okay sweetie, time to road test the skills you've learned in therapy," and sent her off at daybreak to confront her ghosts. Ellie turned up the heat in the car and tried to fend off a lonely feeling that hovered between dread and anticipation. Her ostensible destination was the Finger Lakes, a trip she'd made hundreds of times. She knew every inch of the terrain, but today her goal was the uncharted landscape within herself.

An hour later, as she drove through Newark, pale sun shone on the dreary outside world, but she had company inside the car—her husband and son. She could see them, hear them, smell them, feel the warmth of them. She'd spent the last five months weaving together joy and sorrow, learning to celebrate as she grieved them. Today they would support her as she reached all the way back for memories floating in the half light where she'd hidden them the day her childhood ended.

As she drove, impressions of the past flickered—her brother's legs flashing in dappled light as he raced toward the deep morning blue of the lake, the warm red taste of wild strawberries, her father's voice belting out "Maybe I'm Amazed" while he pounded an old upright piano—but each receded before she could capture it. With continued effort, she mastered the skill of dragging one image and then another into the light and holding it there.

Throughout the second half of her life she'd censored her memories, allowed herself only glimpses of the first half. But within the confines of that small car, for the first time since the death of her father and brother, she fully opened the door to her childhood. Connected joy to the unbearable pain of losing it. By the time Ellie turned onto the path that led to Mark and Jane's house, she'd accepted the ponderous gift of grief that had awaited her for eighteen years.

She sat with Jane and explained her sojourn. "Will thought I was running away from him when I left London, but I wasn't fleeing anything.

I was running toward my past, something Andrew always hoped I'd do. At last I've started, and he's . . . not . . . here to see it." She looked down and caressed her left hand, slowly twisting the wide gold band she'd worn for over ten years. "I'll never replace him. You know that, don't you?" Jane nodded and Ellie said, "But I'm in love with Will."

"Oh honey, Mark and I realized that quite some time ago. We're happy for you."

Four months later, Ellie called from London with exciting news. "Will and I are going to have a baby in March. We're getting married this fall at Will's parents house in Yorkshire. I hope you'll fly to England and help us celebrate."

Almost two years after the death of their son and grandson, Jane and Mark sat in the sun celebrating a wedding breakfast with Ellie's new family. Will's friend Jack tapped his glass and proposed the first toast. "I want to salute the Shakespeare-quoting sheep farmer I met the day we came up to Oxford. He had never held a squash racquet, but he was keen to learn. In twenty years, his enthusiasm never flagged. He never stopped competing even though I regularly humiliated him on the court. Last week he bested me four days in a row." A grin flitted across Jack's face. "If that's what impending fatherhood does for one's game, I may give it a go." He raised his mimosa. "To Will, the finest mate a man could have."

Jane's toast was last. "My tribute is a kind of complement to Jack's. Fifteen years ago, our son Andrew wrote from London, describing the bright, tender-hearted girl he'd met. He said Ellie was devoted to Shakespeare and had never heard of squash, the only ballgame he ever played. He brought her home to meet Mark and me, and she became our daughter. We lost Andrew and our grandson, Danny, two years ago. A year later, Ellie moved back to London where she met and fell in love with a squash-playing Shakespeare enthusiast . . . Chance? Fate? . . . Whichever it was, I feel they're completing a circle, and Andrew would be cheering them on." She lifted her glass. "To our daughter, Ellie, and our new son, Will. To family."

LAST WORDS

2009

I lost my father and younger brother to a fire when I was seventeen. My mother to cancer, eight years later. Instead of coming to terms with the deaths, with my role as a surviver, I buried the past deep inside myself and carried on. By age thirty I had a husband and a son I adored, I loved my job, I laughed a lot. I was happy—in the daytime. But sometimes at night, angst would rise up and threaten to dismantle my life. My husband would listen to my rambling worries, then console me back to sleep. One night he said, "You miss your father and mother, but it's the departure of your brother that afflicts you like an unhealed wound. You're obsessed by a fear that he was overwhelmed by regret at the moment of his death, and by your own feelings of guilt for having survived. You've lost connection to the happiness you shared with him."

He gave me an assignment. "Sometime when you're wide awake, I want you to dwell on everything you loved about your brother. Bring him to life in your mind, and contemplate that living boy confronting death. Take as much time as you need. Then write the last words he might have spoken. Don't write until you've come to an honest place."

It took years and two more heartbreaking deaths—my husband's and our son's—but I eventually landed where I needed to be. I was ready. I sat and began to write my brother's words.

"The Rest Is Silence"

On my last day—in the fire—in the moment before I died, I knew Dad and I were leaving the world of the living. The final instant before my death was an eternity. All pain had passed, and I could see my whole life, more clearly than I can explain to a living person. Could remember everything I'd ever done, every thought I'd had, every word anyone had spoken to me. Each happy moment I'd experienced and each sad one throbbed to the same rhythm within me. And though I couldn't see the future, what would happen to my mom and my sister, I could feel their sadness at losing me. I knew I couldn't erase their sorrow, and I accepted that. More than anything, I wished they could know I was going to be okay. Better than okay. Not missing anyone. Free from all pain, in a way that they weren't. But I wasn't worried about them. I knew that someday, somehow, they'd figure it out.

The threshold of death was an amazing place. My capacity for perception was greater than it had been in the midst of life. Everyone I'd ever met was there with me. They filled the expanse of my mind, stretching to its furthest reaches, yet as close to me as they could be. They were spiritual beings with neither bodies nor faces, but I recognized each of them.

My love for my family and friends was more profound than it had been just minutes before. I forgave myself every wrong I'd committed during my life and pardoned each person who had hurt me.

I had always thought death would be frightening, and as the flames approached, I was afraid. But in that infinite final instant before I died, I was fearless. I saw that the void was not empty. It was filled with peace. I knew the truth—"The rest is silence."

The story of the moment of my brother's death seemed to come straight from him. For years as I tried to sort my feelings, I had been confused and tormented, but as I wrote, his words flowed like a river and washed away my cares. When I finished writing, he read them with me. His newly deep adolescent voice harmonized with mine, and together we spoke for him and our father and mother. For my husband and son. Eighteen years after my brother's death, I finally laid him to rest.

PIECES OF MY LIFE

2009

L ast night, I dreamed about my family—my husband and son. This morning, the silvery notes of a child's laughter floated up amidst the sounds of Brooklyn traffic and through my bedroom window. *Danny's here.* I open my eyes. I'm alone.

Downstairs, the reflexive steps of coffee-making—the smell of the beans, the whir of the grinder, the rush of steam from the kettle, the dark taste of Italian roast—open me up. I walk with my cup and the swirl of my mixed emotions, to the living room where I stand remembering life in this house. The years with Andrew and Danny are the only ones that count. After they died, I lost myself, lost almost a year. When I finally awoke from the stupor of those missing months, I gathered up photos of people I loved, and carried them to London, where I'd met

Andrew fourteen years earlier. Without my husband and our son, I was no longer a wife and mother. I spent five months in the city—figuring out what I was, who I was. A one hundred and fifty-day education in widowhood. Coming back to New York was a journey into my past. At last, I'm ready for the present. Next week I'll return to London and to Will, the man who guided me through every intersection as I walked my way back to life.

He flew to New York last week and helped me sort Andrew's study and Danny's bedroom. I touched every item each of them had owned, wept as I told him their stories. The tangible results of that journey filled two boxes. Pieces I'll want to touch again and again—an old magnifying glass, a tee shirt silkscreened by a four-year-old's hand, a pair of size five red and white striped pajamas, a squash racket, Andrew's beloved *Essential Epicurus,* and Danny's *Charlotte's Web.* Remnants of their lives, of my life with them. At the last moment, I pulled a faded yellow and blue quilt from a chest in the entry hall and handed it to Will.

"Which box?" he asked, "Andrew's or Danny's?"

"I'm not sure. Neither of them ever saw it. It was my brother's. I hadn't come to terms with his death. I couldn't bring myself to touch it."

"And now you have, and you can."

"Right. Put it in Danny's box."

I've made a firm decision. I'm moving to London with nothing but my memories and the two boxes Will and I packed. Tomorrow the house and every material thing left in it goes up for sale. I touch the sofa we napped on, remember the forts Danny built with its cushions. Look around at paintings Andrew and I bought together, a hand-thrown bowl on the coffee table, an exquisite vase on the dining room sideboard. Beautiful things, but just things. I'll remember them, miss them, but I won't need them. Every item is replaceable.

My eyes rest on the blanket chest. My mother loved the battered antique. Made a dying request that I keep it. And I have, for ten years. But Mom was a practical woman. She wouldn't have expected me to pack up the old chest and send it across the Atlantic.

I lift the lid. It's empty, had held nothing but my brother's quilt. I tug on the wide, shallow lower drawer, diligently working it back and forth until it's partially open. I can see something written in faded ink across its bottom but can't make out the words. I'm suddenly determined to read the inscription. It's the least I can do before selling off this piece of my past. I jerk the drawer to the left, then the right—until it's all the way out—carry it to a window and read the words. "To my wife, Nell, with love from Emmet, on the occasion of our wedding, 16 May 1925, Cork City, Ireland."

"Oh my god, this belonged to Dad's mother." As a child I'd known that my dad was born in Ireland, but my parents had carefully wrapped their personal stories in a parcel and set it out of reach of my brother and me.

Everything I know about my family's past, I learned one afternoon the week before my mom died. She told me the story of having been disowned by her parents, a painful burden she'd shared with no one but my dad, and attempted to fill in the details of my dad's life—his father's death in Dublin, followed by a move from Ireland to Brooklyn with his mom and older brother, the loss of his mother when he was only four years old.

I replace the drawer and run my hand over the worn golden wood of the chest, thinking of all the hands that have touched it since the day my father's father, my son's great-grandfather, wrote those words to his wife-to-be. I contemplate the history lost in the muddle of family secrets. My grandmother, a widow with two boys, managed to carry the heavy chest with her when she sailed from Ireland to Brooklyn. My father would have known its story. He took it with him when he moved up to the Finger Lakes and lived with it until the day he died. Mom cared for it in his memory for the next eight years, and after her death, I brought it back to Brooklyn.

I step back for another look. It stands where we placed it ten years ago. I've walked by it thousands of times. Dusted it, left Andrew notes on it, gathered up the remains of abandoned Lego structures. But today, for the first time, I see it. The chest is a story connecting my past to the present and the future. It tells a truth I'm still learning. Andrew used to say, "When your heart tells you to ignore a firm decision you've made, listen."

I won't sell this piece of my life to a stranger. I grab my phone and call the shipping company I contracted to move my two boxes. "I'm Ellinor O'Neal Campbell. I want to amend an order I made last Thursday. I have a blanket chest I want to ship to London. It's irreplaceable."

FOUR MINUTES—IF
YOU PLAY IT TWICE

2010

A pounding rain overflowed the gutters of the Yorkshire cottage and wind rattled its windows, but the noise of the early spring deluge was hard pressed to compete with the words of "And Your Bird Can Sing" that blared from the kitchen CD player. The bright music lit up the grey morning. Sophie sang along with Lennon and McCartney. When the singing gave way, she played air guitar with George Harrison. Her son burst into the room. "Mum, why are you playing the tea song today?"

"Remember what's happening this afternoon? Will and Ellie are coming to visit, and they're bringing your cousin, baby Lizzie."

"Oh yeah, so this time it's for a happy reason, right?"

"Right, Charlie." Only five years old, he already knew the drill. Understood the music's role. How the driving beat of the whimsical song served to alleviate dreariness or amplify a celebration.

As a child, Sophie had impatiently counted the months till her birthday, the days till her weekly trip to the sweet shop. "I can hardly bear to wait," she'd say. Even the four minutes required to bring tea to its peak of flavor seemed interminable. "Why does tea have to sit in the pot so long before we can drink it? It's boring."

Her father concocted the "And Your Bird Can Sing" ritual as a light-hearted and productive way for Sophie to pass those minutes. "As soon as I pour the water," he said, "you place the needle on the record just so. Sing the words and play a make-believe guitar along with Paul McCartney and George Harrison. Finish off by playing that last long riff. Then start the song again. While it plays the second time, lay out the cups and spoons and sugar and milk and biscuits. When the Beatles play their last chord, the tea will be perfect." Her ingenious father had calculated how long it would take his five-year-old daughter to lay the table and precisely coordinated the music with the activity. Four minutes—if you played the song twice.

At age thirty-nine, Sophie was no longer impatient. Minutes—even years—seemed to fly by. She couldn't remember the last time she'd been bored. But the music of the childhood ritual still played a role in her life. Evoking memories. Cheering her when she was feeling down. Enhancing anticipation of events like her niece's first visit to Yorkshire.

The kettle began to whistle, and Charlie held an imaginary guitar aloft. "Would you like me to play?"

"I would. I'll start the music again as soon as I've poured the water, then you go for it." Charlie sang every word and played with a vengeance for two minutes. He finished his performance with a flourish, and Sophie pushed restart. Together they laid the table with cups and spoons and sugar and milk and biscuits while the song filled the room again.

"Do you think we should play it for Lizzie this afternoon?"

"I do." They sat down to their perfect tea. "It's a family tradition."

WAY BETTER THAN
SLEEPING

2012

On the first day of June, two weeks before her thirty-eighth birth-day, Ellie completed a Bachelor of Science in psychology in preparation for the postgraduate programme she would begin at the end of summer. Her husband, Will, hugged her. "You have three months off. How do you plan to spend your first free weekend?"

She didn't hesitate for a second. "That's a no-brainer. All I want is sleep, as much as my body needs."

At five the next morning, their two-year-old, Lizzie, crept into Ellie and Will's bed. They snuggled her between them and were asleep again within minutes.

Two hours later, Will awoke and gazed at his family—Ellie asleep on her back and Lizzie straddling the mound of her mum's belly. London's late spring sun slipped between the slats of the venetian blinds and cast bars of light across the two of them. He marveled at the beauty of his wife, her serene face surrounded by the splendid gold tangle of her hair, with one baby inside her and another on top of her. In less than a month Lizzie would have a brother. They'd call him Jack, for Will's best friend of twenty-four years.

Ellie groaned softly and kissed her daughter's dark curls. "I have to go to the bathroom, sweetie."

"I'll go too." Lizzie scrambled off the bed and ran across the room ahead of her mum. Minutes later, she skipped back to her parents' bed. "Hurray! Hurray! Our baby is going to get born today."

Will sat up with a start. "What?"

"She's right." Ellie's voice was vibrant. "I think he's going to be a speedy little guy. I just had a fairly strong contraction. They may have started while I slept."

"How far apart are they?"

"I can't tell. I've only been awake for this one. We can start timing when I have another."

"Should we call the midwife?"

"No-o, let's not get ahead of ourselves. Why don't you call Jack and arrange for him or Rose to come round sometime this morning and collect Lizzie."

The little girl frowned. "Why does Uncle Jack collect me? I want to see our baby get born."

"Mum and Daddy are going to be busy getting ready for the baby," Ellie said. "Jack and Rose will bring you back home to see him as soon as he's born."

"Can I hold him?"

"Of course you can. Will, another one's beginning. Start the stopwatch. Then call Jack . . . and your parents. They'll want to be in the loop."

Will set the watch and pressed Jack's number. He took a quick breath. "Ellie's started labor. Can you or Rose come round for Lizzie in an hour or two?"

"You sound shaken, mate. You were more laid back than this last time."

"You're right. I am a little shaky. This situation is entirely different. Lizzie was born in a hospital. This birth's going to be at home. It's all down to us. And he's coming almost two weeks early."

"Lighten up, Will. I've known you for over twenty years. A challenge brings out the best in you. You're certainly ready for this one. You have a midwife, and you're working with Ellie, who's bound to have sorted every detail."

Will paced as he rang his mother. Relieved when she didn't pick up, he attempted a positive tone on the voice mail he left. "Mum, it's eight o'clock Saturday morning. Ellie's labor has started. You and dad are likely to have a new grandson before the day is up. We're hoping you'll be able to make the drive to London. Give us a call."

Four contractions later, Jack walked through the front door and kissed Ellie. "You're looking radiant." He regarded her blue Tottenham Hotspur shirt and grey workout pants. "And your fashion choice is stunningly appropriate for the work you'll be doing today." He thumped Will on the back and swept Lizzie up in his arms. "Aunt Rose is home making shortbread hearts. Let's go help her."

Will wouldn't let Ellie out of his sight. He followed her from room to room as she picked up toys, reshelved books, watered plants. Occasionally she'd embrace her belly and speak to the baby inside her. She glowed with delight. Her worldview was simple: "You never know what the future holds, so celebrate every happy moment you're allotted." At the start of each contraction, she alerted Will with an enthusiastic thumbs-up. He'd reset the stopwatch.

"I'm bloody useless," he said. "You're blithely cleaning the house between contractions, and all I do is pace the floor."

"You are not useless. You're making phone calls, timing the contractions, serving me tea. That's all I want right now. Conserve your heroism. I may need it later."

Carolyn, Will's mother, called at eleven. "I left my phone in the car overnight, and I just got your message. How is Ellie?"

"She's fine, Mum. She's swept and scrubbed every floor in the house. At this moment, she's chopping herbs for an omelette. We're looking forward to seeing you and Dad. How soon can you take off?"

Ellie called from the kitchen, "Tell them our little boy is in a hurry, and he's going to want to see his grandparents when he-u-uh-" Her voice rose. "O-o-h." She inhaled deeply and let her breath slide out.

"Mum, I've got to go. We'll talk later."

When the contractions were eight minutes apart, Will called Julia, the midwife. "Is Ellie comfortable?" she asked. "Is she calm?"

"Oh yeah. At the moment, she's sitting on that big ball in our birthing room, singing along to 'Let it Be.' Between contractions, she cooks and cleans. She's totally chuffed. But I'm stressed. The baby's coming early, and I've read about all the problems that can accompany premature births."

"I'm happy for Ellie, but you must stop worrying, Will. I have her dates in front of me. The baby's coming one week and a day early. Tomorrow will be thirty-nine weeks, and that's not premature. You need to stop fretting and concentrate on the strengths you bring to the table. You came to this process having observed and helped at your daughter's birth. You were the star pupil in our Birthing for Fathers classes. And Ellie told me you started lambing sheep up north before you were twelve. Not quite like helping your wife give birth to a son, of course, but someone composed enough to do that as a pre-teen can certainly locate his tranquil center at age forty. Got that?" She paused. "Now relax and call back when her contractions are five minutes apart."

An hour and a half later, Will rang Julia again. "They are coming every five minutes. Each one is lasting so long, Ellie's barely getting a rest, and her water just broke."

"I'm on my way. The drive should take me twenty minutes. I'll be there by one thirty."

Will helped Ellie out of her soggy workout pants. As he watched her, inundated by waves of pain that seemed to wrap themselves around her, empathy displaced his anxiety.

Julia rang fifteen minutes later. "I'm stopped in traffic on High Gate Road. At this point nothing's moving at all." Her voice was calm. "If I were there, I'd check Ellie's cervix. I would like you to do it. You saw a PowerPoint in class, but I can give you a verbal refresher right now if you need one."

Will was no longer nervous. "I don't need a refresher. I can do it. By the way, you have our friend Jack's phone number. I'd appreciate your ringing him. We could use an extra pair of hands."

"Great idea. I'll get in touch with him right now. Congratulations, Will. I believe you've recovered your serenity."

He tweaked the truth a bit for Ellie. "Julia's been slightly delayed; she wants me to check your cervical dilation. Let's get it done quickly before she gets here."

Unrelenting pain was sapping Ellie's strength. Her voice shook a little. "She'll be here soon?"

He had no idea when Julia would arrive, so he expressed his hope. "Yes, soon." He gently eased Ellie into a squatting position and selected what he needed from a sideboard stocked with bin bags, towels, disinfectants, latex gloves.

"Here we go." With a sanitized and gloved hand and his newly reclaimed self-confidence, Will began the exam. It took less than a minute. "You're just shy of ten centimeters. I could feel our baby's head." Ellie tried to speak, but her words morphed into a groan. She knelt on the floor beside the bed and supported herself on her forearms.

Will had quit counting minutes. Oblivious of passing time, he massaged Ellie's back and wiped the sweat from her face. A door slammed below. The sound of heavy footfalls on the stairs followed, and Jack exploded into the room. He threw out his hands. "What shall I do first?"

"You can get Ellie a fresh shirt while I call the midwife. We need her on speaker talking us through this." He pressed Julia's number and waited for her to pick up.

Jack bantered with Ellie as he tugged the sweat-drenched shirt over her head. "Seeing you nude is a bonus I wasn't expecting."

Ellie glared at him. "Not funny." She slid a lock of damp hair behind her ear. "I look wretched."

Will and Jack protested in unison, "You look beautiful."

At the trill of a ringtone in the hallway, the three of them turned toward the door. Julia burst through it and silenced her phone. "That was your call, Will." She hurried to Ellie, knelt and rubbed her back. "You're doing incredibly well, dear." She looked up at the two men. "You all are."

"She was at almost ten centimeters when I checked," Will said.

Julia radiated cheerful confidence. "Wonderful. Firstly, I'm going to listen to baby's heart." She pressed the Pinard against Ellie's abdomen. "135 beats per minute. Excellent. And now I'll have a look with a mirror." She moved Ellie's leg to one side. "Oh my, he's so close. Almost here. Do you want to see him?"

Ellie nodded and looked in the mirror. "It's Jackie," she whispered before moaning in pain.

"It is," Julia said, "and he's almost ready to greet you. You keep taking those shallow breaths. Then at my signal, hold tight to Will's and Jack's hands and push. Would you like a puff of gas and air?"

"No, I don't need one." Ellie looked up at Will. "This is way better than sleeping."

Ten grueling minutes later, Julia guided the slippery infant out into the world and placed him in his father's waiting arms, then helped his exhausted, elated mother up onto the bed. Will kissed the squalling newborn and laid him on Ellie's abdomen. "Take a look at your lovely mum." The baby ceased crying and locked eyes with Ellie. Dug in his feet and slowly inched his way toward the breast he needed. Will and Ellie watched, captivated by his primal quest. After a twenty-minute crawl, he reached his destination and latched on. Will wiped his son's face and head with a warm, damp flannel and tucked a soft coverlet around him. "There you go, little one. You're ready to meet your sister."

"Right," Jack said. "I told Rose to follow me here after half an hour. She'll be waiting downstairs with Lizzie. I'll invite them up."

Lizzie, suddenly shy, entered the room holding tight to Rose's hand. She looked up at Jack, who squatted to face her. "You've been waiting since morning to see your baby. You're a big sister. Go for it, girl." His words did the trick. She let go and ran to the bed where her brother lay in her mum's arms.

Will lifted her, wedged her into the crook of Ellie's left elbow, and placed her small hand on the blanket that swaddled the tiny boy. He stepped back to admire his wife with her two babies. *A sublime image of maternity. I want a record.* He pulled out his phone. Going for the perfect shot, he aimed, backed up, then zoomed.

Before he could determine the correct composition, Lizzie, fully recovered from her bout of timidity, called out, "Hurry, Dad, we have a new baby in this family. Come help us hold him."

Jack reached for the phone. "Give it to me. Lizzie's right. It's a family portrait. You belong in it."

Will slipped off his shoes, crawled onto the bed beside Lizzie, and embraced his wife and children.

As Julia put the finishing touches on her cleanup, she appraised the happy group. "Jack, I have a feeling that you and Rose are a vital part of this family. You two stand, one on either side of the bed, and I'll take the photo." She pointed the camera at the joyful faces that surrounded the nursing baby, shot without hesitation, and assessed the result. "It's brilliant." She handed the phone back to Will. "When there's this much love in a room, you can't take a bad picture."

THE MORE WE
GIVE . . .

2016

Hampstead, London, UK

December 18, 2016

Dear Jane and Mark,

What a year this has turned out to be. In my worst moments, I fear the world is going straight to hell. The results of the Brexit referendum here and the presidential election in the States have taxed my reserve of optimism. Even Will, whose social justice work is fueled by a fervent belief in the human capacity for good, struggles with doubts these days.

In the midst of this distress, I pause to appreciate my personal good luck in having married Andrew. In having you as parents-in-law, who stood by me through my long winter of desolation after his and Danny's death, who welcomed Will as a son, and who have embraced our children. It's comforting to think of you back there at home, surrounded by fields readied for winter. Where, despite the 24-hour news cycle, farm life is proceeding as it always has. It's our family's relationship with you, who tend the natural world and heed its calendar, that keeps us balanced.

I'm writing to tell you of a life change we're about to make for the benefit of our family and the community. This past October on the drive home from Yorkshire, while Lizzie and Jack slept, Will and I talked about the elephant in the room—the house we live in. We came to the conclusion that his striving to bring about justice through public policy while we carried on living in such an upmarket house was at the very least unseemly. Before we reached our front door, we had resolved to put the house on the market and begin a search for a smaller place. We've managed to complete the entire process in under two months. All details have been finalized, and we'll be moving into a terraced house in Primrose Hill the second week in January.

We've spent over four years in this large house that we chose for the grounds surrounding it. We wanted a place where our children could run and climb trees, and they have done that with a passion. We'll all miss the garden, but the children are ideal ages to adapt to using public spaces for outdoor activities. As for the house itself, not a one of us is going to miss the two imposing reception rooms, the four bathrooms, or the dining room that seats sixteen. We'll invest the proceeds from its sale in programs that improve life in this city. To paraphrase Shakespeare, the more we give, the more we have. In 1998, your generosity enabled Andrew and me to purchase a house in Brooklyn. It is that gift that Will and I are now paying forward. Thank you.

We're anticipating the perks of our smaller house. Easier housekeeping—fewer windows to wash and bathrooms to clean. And more important, an expanded outlook for the children. They are totally onboard with the change, and that's down to Will. He's a natural teacher who's using their sense of fair play as a point of departure to present a primary level course in social justice. They're helping us decide how to best utilize our new space. Lizzie has come up with a plan for parceling out the three bedrooms. The largest for her and Jack "because we have two beds," the middle-sized one for Will and me, and the smallest "for when we have overnight guests." Jack is in full agreement with her—a rare state of affairs—regarding the shared room concept. In three weeks, the theoretical will become practical. For all of us. There may be rough patches along the way, but we'll push through them. Together.

So you see, despite the pessimistic words that opened my letter, I do have hope. We'll continue giving thanks for our good fortune and contributing what we can to the greater good.

The spare room will stand ready and waiting for you.

Love always, Ellie

Tompkins County, New York

December 24, 2016

Dear Ellie,

What a pleasure to receive a letter so full of gratitude and resolve and hope. I sometimes think about how much Andrew and Danny would love your new family. Then I'm struck by the realization that it was the tragedy of their death that brought Will and Lizzie and Jack to you, and my thoughts form a knot that's hard to untangle. I imagine Andrew's reaction. In his easygoing way, he'd use a favorite expletive to help me confront the dilemma, would call the situation "a beautiful fucking mystery" and tell me to simply appreciate it. So that's what I try to do.

Mark and I are proud of you and Will. The positive impact you're going to make on your community is sure to bring gratification to you both. And what role models you are for your children! We toast you all as you embark on this journey.

You know how, in memory of Danny, Mark turned our pumpkin patch into a gift for the community. Invited any child to pick a pumpkin free of charge. The satisfaction we both derived from that small gesture led us to donate half of the farm's annual profits to our local food bank. At this stage of life, we don't need the income. I don't have a mind full of Shakespeare like you do, Ellie, but I know we are richer for what we give away.

It may be a while before we can take advantage of the guest room in your new home, but please do keep it ready for us. In the meantime, have fun exploring the neighborhood. As I recall, you can view the immensity of London from atop Primrose Hill. Jack and Lizzie can text Mark and me photos of the panorama.

Love to you and all the family, Jane

SECRETS

2017

Part I

Ellie Bonham, a grief therapist who had lost five family members by age thirty-three, was passionate about her work and her family. Each weekday, she was out the door at six thirty before her husband, Will, and their two children were awake. She saw eight patients between seven and three, then switched gears and picked up Lizzie and Jack from school at three thirty. The second Friday in October, before heading home to take care of last minute laundry, she stopped at Tesco where each child picked out a veggie lunch pack for the next day's road trip.

The family spent spring and autumn half-term holidays in the Yorkshire Dales with Will's parents. They loved life in London, but two working parents and two active children made for a hectic schedule. The time up north was easy and unstructured, a breath of fresh air. For seven bliss-ful days twice a year, Ellie and Will scarcely looked at a clock.

The tradition was about to be modified. Will was chairing a confer-ence on the pro-Brexit referendum's impact on immigrants and wouldn't make the trip with the family. His original plan had been to go up for two days, but as the weekend approached, he realized he couldn't do. He told the children on Thursday night, "I'd be distracted, nervous, and no fun whatsoever."

"Dad, you're never nervous," Jack said.

Lizzie grabbed her dad's hand. "That's right, and being with Gran and Granddad is always fun."

Will, usually a soft touch, didn't relent. "Not this time. I have too much on my plate." He squatted and looked at them face to face. "But I'll make up for it next spring. You know that, don't you?" Lizzie nodded at her father, then fixed her eyes on Jack until he followed her lead.

Will helped load the car and waved a regretful goodbye as his family set out after a late breakfast on Saturday. Jack waved until his dad was out of sight. "He already looks lonely. He's going to be sorry he didn't come with us. I just know it."

"You'll have lots of fun to report when we get back home. He'll love hearing about it. Dad's going to be fine," Ellie said.

She wasn't sure she would be. It was her first trip to Yorkshire with-out Will. She was missing his company before she even reached the M1, but as she drove she began to appreciate what the day was offering. She and the children spent plenty of time together, but the parameters of this situation were unique: one adult, two children, a confined space, and four hours. Lizzie and Jack had her full attention when they wanted it, but she receded and listened silently when they didn't seek her out. The children laughed and argued and taunted and forgave each other. *I'm going to learn something on this trip.*

It was after three when she turned onto the lane that led to Will's parents' cottage. Jack reached up between the seats for her phone. "May I call? So they'll be ready?"

"Yes, I think they'd like that."

The two children unhooked their seat belts in anticipation and leapt out when the car came to a stop. Their grandmother, slender and lithe at age seventy-three, ran toward the two of them and gathered them together in one large hug. "Granddad has tea waiting for us. Let's hurry." They held hands and skipped along the path to the house. Ellie stood still and watched. She'd never known her grandparents, never felt that bond. Experiencing Will's parents, Carolyn and Greg, through her children's eyes was an ever-evolving delight.

The weather was warm for October. Dahlias and roses still sparkled, and the children basked in the sun and the luxury of rural freedom for five days. One afternoon, Ellie and Carolyn met Will's sister, Sophie, for tea in the village while Jack and Lizzie wandered along High Street with their cousin, Charlie, exploring shops without adult intervention. Her children relished the sort of independence they weren't allowed in London, but they were happiest at the farm, following their granddad and his two collies through the hills that bordered the property. Each day as the sun began to set, the five Bonhams, wrapped in the fullness of family, ate together under the pergola. The week without Will was going better than Ellie had expected.

Friday morning, clouds rolled in and the skies opened up. Carolyn peered out at the rain pelting the windows and pouring from the gutters. "I guess we'll have tea inside by the fire today."

Jack went to the bedroom and came out with an iPad. "Mum, may I play Harry Potter? I haven't played for five days. I want to teach Grand-dad, okay?"

"Sure."

"If Jack can play on the tablet, I can go online, right? I want to do research," Lizzie said.

"Research?" Jack scoffed. "You think you're so big, but you're only seven. You don't know how to do research."

"Yes, I do. Not like Mum and Dad, but I can look things up about Yorkshire. That's research, isn't it?"

"It is," Ellie said. "Share your websites with one of the adults."

"Right, Mum. I know." She pulled a face. "I have to be safe."

Ellie had spent most of the week outside, scrambling over brackeny hills, watching the dogs herd Lizzie and Jack, loving every breath of country air. She'd planned to bike to the village with the two of them that afternoon and was more disappointed by the unrelenting rain than they were.

"Let Greg and me mind the children for a few hours," Carolyn said. "Close your door and have some personal time." Ellie carried a cup of tea to her room and picked up *Grief is the Thing with Feathers*, the little novel Will had given her to read on holiday.

"It's so short, you'll finish it in an hour," he'd said. "Don't put it off though. You'll want to read it a second time, maybe even a third." Every morning she'd wake up, look at the book on the nightstand and think, *Tonight.* But each evening she was asleep within minutes of kissing Jack and Lizzie goodnight.

Ellie leaned back and opened the book. *At last.* The extraordinary prose swept her away to the London flat of a dad and two boys in mourn-ing. She had reached the father's *never agains*—a variation of the list that haunted her and every other survivor—when Lizzie burst through the door and displaced the dirge.

"Mum, guess what I discovered—an indoor climbing wall in Harrogate. Like the sports centre where I went with my class. I looked up the weather. It's going to rain again tomorrow. I'd love to have a climb there. Please, Mum. It'll be good for me, healthier than being online. Jack can join us if he wants to."

"No promises yet. Show me the page so I can read about it." Lizzie ran from the room and returned a minute later carrying the laptop. The brightly colored website was filled with information about climbing classes for every skill level. It was definitely a kid-friendly venue. "It looks good. We'll need to sign you up for a class. Ask Jack how he feels about rock climbing."

"I already did. He wants to stay and work with Granddad. But I really want to give it a go."

Saturday dawned greyer and wetter than Friday. Ellie and Lizzie left the farm after breakfast and within an hour had found a parking space close to the entrance of the climbing centre. They clasped hands and ran laughing through the deluge. Raindrops clung to Lizzie's eyelashes and dripped from her nose. She looked up and sang, "I love this day."

She beamed as they hired shoes and equipment for her. "This is my second time climbing," she told the assistant helping her. "I had one class in London. I was quite good. The coach said I was a natural." Ellie watched with pride and amusement as Lizzie began scaling the wall. She was a bold child, nothing like Will or herself or Jack. The three of them stood back and assessed any new situation, then stepped in cautiously— if at all. Lizzie jumped in with abandon and learned on the fly.

Ellie was lost in the moment, watching her resolute, smiling daughter when a crisp voice rang out over the boisterous clamor of the room. "Will, we need to be going."

She turned and saw the speaker—a fit, raven-haired woman dressed in climbing clothes—looking up at a boy who responded from high on the wall, "Mum, please, a few more minutes. Please, Mum?"

"All right, fifteen minutes more, but that's all. We're to meet Dad in half an hour."

A spark of recognition flared in Ellie's mind. She remembered Will's description of Kate, his intrepid, cliff-climbing, horse-riding former wife. "Slender and athletic, with rosy cheeks and hair that shines like a blackbird's wing."

Ellie's emotions regarding the woman had run the gamut—from outrage to jealousy to amazement. "I'm impressed," she'd said when Will described how he'd galloped over the moors with her.

He'd given a modest shrug. "I wasn't very impressive."

"Not by you. By her—for getting you to ride a horse across the moors. I think I'd like to meet her."

Ultimately, she'd forgotten about Kate, but seeing this woman who so matched her husband's description—and who had a son called Will—piqued her curiosity. *Perhaps fate has brought us together today.* She glanced at Lizzie, intent at her task and heedless of a parental audience. With a racing heart, she turned and approached the woman who had called out to her son. "Excuse me."

"Yes, may I help you?"

"I-I'm not sure. I'm wondering, is your name Kate?"

The woman's reply was as much an inquiry as an affirmation. "Yes?"

"I have another question."

"All right. Ask."

"Were you once married to Will Bonham?"

The woman's face softened slightly. "I was."

"You caught my attention when you called out to your son. And when your appearance matched Will's description of you, I decided to speak. I'm his wife, Ellie. I used to fantasize about meeting you, but that was years ago. I haven't thought about you in a long time. And of course, you've never thought of me."

"Oh, but I have. Once, quite a while ago. A friend of my father-in-law who was at your wedding told me Will had married an American girl, that you two were expecting a baby and were as happy as any newly-weds he'd ever seen. Robert, my husband, felt I should take the wedding and your coming baby as an excuse to call and congratulate Will, but I couldn't do. I didn't think it would be appropriate."

Ellie's heart had stopped racing. "Actually, it would have been appropriate and welcome."

Kate looked away briefly, then clapped eyes on Ellie. "I guess you probably know part of the story. How I left, remarried, and had a baby, without so much as a second thought." She paused. "There was more to it, though. I did try to talk to Will once after my son was born, but I handled it badly—almost indecently—according to my mother."

Ellie's response was gentle. "I know about your attempt to connect with Will. He told me how much it had angered him. He was still hurting far too much to socialize with the man you'd married. When the hurt subsided, he was simply baffled. Your invitation perplexed him for years before he finally put it to rest and let it be."

Kate scrutinized Ellie. "Mmm. I can quite imagine Will with you." She looked at her watch. "I have a few minutes. If you do, I can tell you a bit more of the story."

Ellie looked up at Lizzie, climbing with single-minded determination. "I'd like that." She pointed at a bench that faced the climbing wall. "Let's sit."

Kate's first words were composed, almost brisk. "I blindsided Will when I told him I was leaving and moving back to Yorkshire. I loved him. I really did, but not enough. Not enough to spend my life in London. I was confused while he and I were breaking up, and I leaned on Robert, a childhood friend. There was nothing romantic about the relationship until the divorce was final, but it proceeded quite quickly afterwards. We married within weeks. Getting pregnant immediately was an accident."

Her tempo slowed slightly. "I felt guilty about the pregnancy because I'd put Will off when he wanted a baby so badly. But the birth of my little boy brought me clarity. I looked at him and realized that unconsciously I'd known it wasn't in me to raise a child in the center of London. I simply couldn't have done. I wasn't at fault; nor was Will."

Her voice dropped to just above a whisper. "Will was the first man I ever loved. We were together for six significant years—I grew up with him. I wanted to name my son in honor of what he and I had shared, and Robert supported my wish." She looked down at her hands, folded tightly in her lap. "I thought if Will came round and met my husband and our baby, I could explain why I'd had to leave him, and he'd understand." Her face crumpled.

Ellie reached for her hand. "Thank you. It's gracious of you to tell me this story at a moment's notice. I truly appreciate it. You and Will were good for each other for a while. That's what Carolyn told me years ago. Being good for one another is the best we can hope for in a relationship, isn't it?"

Lizzie ran toward them. For a second, Ellie was sorry to have missed part of the climb, but the exultation shining on her daughter's face washed away any regret she might have felt. "Lizzie, I've been talking to Kate. She's an old friend of Dad's."

"It's a pleasure to meet you, Lizzie." Kate's voice was warm, but the little girl offered only a solemn look and a barely polite dip of her head. "Well, I've got to collect my son and go to lunch. Very good to have met you both." The boy, a lanky teen, reached the foot of the wall. "Come on, Will," she called. "Dad's waiting for us." He ran up and offered a quick smile before the two of them walked away.

Ellie reached for her daughter's hand. "Okay, let's go home and tell everyone about your climb."

A frown clouded Lizzie's face. "You touched that woman's arm." It was an accusation. "Who was she really? She wasn't Dad's friend." Her voice cracked. "She was his wife, wasn't she?"

The statement bewildered Ellie. She and Will had discussed telling the children about his first marriage but hadn't yet decided on the right moment. "Yes, she was. We've never talked about that though. How did you know?"

Tears welled up in Lizzie's eyes. "Remember when Charlie visited us last summer? The afternoon you and Jack went to the community center, we stayed home and he said Kate's name to me. That she used to be Dad's wife. I told him I didn't believe it." Her next words poured out in an anxious rush. "But it was a lie. I actually did, and I was sick in the ground floor loo. Charlie helped me clean up. He felt really guilty for telling a family secret, and I was scared. Everyone always says 'Lizzie never cries,' but I cried in my bed that night—more than one night—because I was worried about you and Dad. I never said a word to anyone. I was afraid I'd make our whole family sad."

Ellie draped her arm over her daughter's shoulder and pulled her close. "O-oh, Lizzie, I'm sorry you had to carry that burden, to keep such a big secret."

"Did you know all about it?"

"I did."

Tears slid down Lizzie's cheeks. She took a determined breath. "And the boy, Will, is he my brother?"

"No, honey. Kate has a new husband. He's the boy's father."

Lizzie sniffled. "Good. I'm glad. It's strange that she named her son after our dad though."

"It is, rather, but she had her reasons. Are you okay?"

"For a while I wasn't, but I have been for quite a long time. I decided if it was really true, Dad would tell me someday, so I would wait until he was ready. I hid what Charlie said in the back of my mind. But you always tell us, 'Listen to the little voice inside you,' and today the voice told me it was time to say what I knew. Do you think Dad's ready to tell me the truth now?"

"I do. Should I ask him to talk to you?"

"No, I think I'm big enough to ask him myself. Do you agree?"

"Yes, Lizzie, I agree."

"May I ask him everything I'm wondering about?"

"Of course you may."

"And what about Jack? Is he old enough to know?"

"What do you think?"

"I think he is. He can listen when Dad talks to me. We both deserve to know the truth. It's our family story. No more secrets."

Part II

Lizzie stood on the hearth touching faces of the photos that lined the mantel. "Dad, we could call this our family tree, right?"

"Mmm, I suppose we could," Will said without looking up from *The Guardian*.

"Do you think we should have a picture of Kate here?"

He put the paper down and turned to his daughter. "No, I do not."

"She used to be part of our family. She used to be your wife. You used to love her."

"Listen to your words. *Used to* is the operative phrase. What you're saying is that she's not part of our family, she is not my wife, that I no longer love her. Therefore, she doesn't belong on our family tree."

"But we have a picture of Andrew. He's not Mum's husband any more."

"Lizzie, you're being obtuse. Andrew died. Mum does still love him. He's the father of Danny, your mother's son, your brother. I hope you're not about to question Danny's place on our family tree."

He immediately regretted the remark. Lizzie's half brother had died before she was born, and she cherished his story. She cast her eyes down. "I'm sorry, Dad. I have a lot of questions in my mind."

Will stood up and pulled her to him. "No. I'm sorry. I should be the one to apologize. Your questions are important. Keep asking them."

She grinned. "Yeah, I will. I always do." She walked to the mantel and continued her examination of the photos. "I already have another one. Everyone has four grandparents—except for Jack and me. We have six because of Danny." She turned over a faded wedding portrait and studied the words inscribed on the back. "But there are only these two, Emmet and Nell O'Neal, for Mum. Where are her other grandparents?"

"Now you've got me. You're going to have to ask her."

———◆———

Will turned out his reading light as Ellie got into bed. "Did Lizzie interrogate you about the absence of certain photos on the mantel when you got home tonight?"

"Yes, quite thoroughly. She had questions I couldn't answer. When I told her my maternal grandmother's name might have been Helene and that I didn't know my grandfather's name, she was indignant. 'How could a person not know the names of her own grandparents for absolutely certain?' "

"Well, you couldn't have handled the situation worse than I did. I was reading an opinion piece in the *Guardian* when she started asking questions about Kate that seemed disingenuous-"

"Disingenuous? Will, she may be precocious, but she's only seven. Even though she seemed to understand your explanation of what happened between you and Kate, she's confused by the notion of divorce. We need to let her express any feelings she has."

"I know, I know. I've admitted I was in the wrong. You haven't heard the worst of it though. I'm sure she didn't repeat my comment about Danny."

"About Danny? No. What did you say?"

"She was rambling on about whether or not Andrew belonged on our family tree. I said I hoped she wasn't about to question Danny's place on it. It was thoughtless of me. I apologized immediately. Told her to keep asking questions."

"That was the right thing for you to say. She will do anyway. It's her default way of being." Ellie paused. "By the way, I do know my grandmother's name 'for absolutely certain.' It was Helene. Lizzie took me by surprise, and for a second I was unsure. But I have no idea of my grandfather's name. Lizzie's right. I should know it." She laid her head against Will's shoulder. "Her questions have moved me closer to an investigation I've been thinking about starting since the day you told the children about your marriage to Kate. I'm about to look inside the one emotional box I've been afraid to open. My mom never spoke of her parents until she was dying. I must have had questions about my grandparents when I was a child, but something kept me from asking them. And I've avoided discovering the answers throughout my adulthood. Mom's secrets had an impact on me—one that lasts until this day. I know next to nothing about my mom's family. It's time I learned more."

———◆———

The next morning, after an hour on the internet, Ellie made a choice and began her search for answers.

eob@hotmail.uk.com   11/2/2017

To info@joyceinvestigativegroup.com

Dear Ms. Joyce:

I understand your team specializes in searches of records of deceased individuals. I am looking for information about Mrs. Helene Johnson who died in Minnesota in October or November of 1991. Mrs. Johnson was the mother of my mother, Mary O'Neal, née Johnson. I would appreciate your help in connecting me with pertinent information and with any living relatives.

Sincerely,

Ellinor Bonham

Frances Joyce <info@joyceinvestigativegroup.com>   11/10/2017

To eob@hotmail.uk.com

Dear Ellinor Bonham:

I have discovered that Mrs. Helene Johnson died in Eldon, Minnesota on October 27, 1991. I have been in contact with her niece, Elisabeth Jensen of St Paul, Minnesota. She has in her possession effects that she is interested in sharing with you. She would welcome an email at eej@gmail.com.

Sincerely,

Frances Joyce

eob@hotmail.uk.com   11/12/2017

To eej@gmail.com

Dear Elisabeth,

Frances Joyce gave me your email address. I'm Helene Johnson's granddaughter. My mother, Mary O'Neal, née Johnson, was estranged from her parents as a young woman and never spoke of them until shortly before her death in 1999.

For years Mom hid the shame of having been rejected by her parents, but at the end of her life, she shared her story and expressed regret for the toll secrets had taken on our family. I discounted the damage secrecy might have inflicted on me and my brother until I began my study of psychotherapy. Even then, for various reasons, I put off delving into Mom's secret. It's my own daughter's curiosity that has prompted me to search for the truth. I want her and my son to know the history of their family. My grandmother and grandfather are part of their story.

During her last days, Mom described the total rejection she'd suffered—how her parents would not allow her to visit their home, wouldn't answer her letters. She had misgivings about her father's love for her but believed that her mother, despite an inability to adequately express maternal feelings, had loved her.

I accept that I will never know the whole story, but if you can enlighten me in any way, I'll greatly appreciate it.

Very best,

Ellie Bonham

Elisabeth Jensen <eej@gmail.com>   11/14/2017

To eob@hotmail.uk.com

Dear Ellie,

Your mother, Mary, was my cousin. I spent happy holidays with her when we were young, but my family's relations with Aunt Helene's family broke down at some point during my childhood. I never knew why. It was all very hush-hush back then.

I know nothing of your grandmother's later life, nor the circumstances of her death. However, I do have a folder labeled "Helene" that I came upon after my own mother passed away in 2002. It contains a sealed envelope meant for Mary Ellinor O'Neal and a studio photograph dated 1953 of Aunt Helene and her husband, Roy, with your mother seated between them.

I believe these items are rightfully yours. I would like to present them to you in person, but given the geographic distance between us, I am willing to mail them to you. Please send me your address in London.

With affection,

Elisabeth

Eight days later a small package arrived in the post. Ellie opened it and studied the black and white photo. A young couple—a dark-eyed brunette woman and a fair-haired, light-eyed man—sat on an old fashioned settee with a blonde child between them. *My mom, probably seven years old, with a toothy grin almost too wide for her little face.* Ellie had seen her mother's smile thousands of times—warm, loving, proud—but she'd never detected that kind of pure joy. She wanted to hug the little girl in the picture and protect her from whatever sadness was to come her way.

She gently traced the curvy letters of the old fashioned script—Mary Ellinor O'Neal—on the manila envelope, then placed it in the top drawer of her desk. She would leave it for a few days. Assess her right to examine contents meant for, but never seen by, her mother. Think about her mom's happiness and her sorrow, the shame she felt at having been rejected by her family, and the persistent hope that her mother had loved her. Reflect on the complex bond between parent and child. Ellie had begun to deal with her relationship to family secrets in the course of her own therapy. She knew something of the role her grandmother had played in the story, but the woman's state of mind was a mystery that hadn't been uncovered. Now it might be.

On Saturday morning, Will took Lizzie and Jack to a children's exhibit at the Museum of London. Ellie had made up her mind. She would honor the memory of her mother and grandmother by opening the sealed envelope. She sat at the desk and reverently removed the pages. With trepidation she began to read.

⬥

Apology to My Daughter

I got a letter from you today, the first one since your father died. I never wrote to tell you he passed away. I don't know how you learned of his death, but I could tell you knew the second I took your letter from the mailbox. It was the only one—since the day he disowned you and banished you from our home—with your address on the envelope. You never included that information while he was alive. Always left the space for the return address blank. I guess you were afraid he'd notice it, that it would set him off.

I carried the sealed envelope up to your old bedroom and sat on the bed where you sat five years ago with tears in your eyes, speaking with a defiance I'd never before heard from you. "Jimmy is the loveliest man I've ever met, and I'm going to marry him."

I was almost afraid to open it. It felt like a real letter, not a card, and I was worried about what you might say. But as soon as I started reading, I could tell you were the same dear Mary. Asking me about the weather and my garden. Inquiring after my health. You have a new baby—that's why you wrote—a beautiful little girl. You named her Ellinor. My mother's name and your middle name, passed down over all these years. You're going to call her Ellie—such a soft sound. It's a thoughtful thing, passing on a name. You've always been like that—kind and considerate—sending me a card every Christmas, a birthday greeting each August, even though I never replied. Maybe you've forgiven me for the role I played that day I put you on a bus back to New York, but I can't forgive myself. Not for any of it.

In your letter you invited me to visit. You want me to know your beautiful baby girl—I can close my eyes and see you pushing her in a pram—and to meet your husband, the man your father rejected for his heritage. I remember with shame the words he shouted that day. "Mary, I gave you every advantage, and you've repaid me by taking up with a low-class Irishman. God knows how someone of his ilk got into a school like Cornell." Such harsh, hurtful words. And I didn't protect you from them.

I'd had to beg your father to let you go out East for graduate school, but your being there gave him bragging rights. "Mary's a real go-getter, a graduate student at an Ivy League college," he'd say every chance he got. You, such a modest girl, would've hated it. Of course my discomfort at his boasting was nothing compared with what I felt when he rejected you for choosing to marry the wrong man. He threw you out of our house. Erased you, our only daughter, from our life. It was devastating, and I was complicit. I am so sorry.

I ask myself every day why I went along with it. I don't think I'll ever understand why, but I couldn't object. It was as if I had no will of my own. I'm ashamed of the way I acted that weekend and for not keeping in touch with you throughout these past years. I've never had the courage to examine my life, let alone share it with you. Today I'm going to try.

My freshman year at St. Cloud, I was more caught up in social life than in academics. Still trying to decide what I'd do after college. I loved children, thought maybe I'd teach kindergarten. I remember saying to myself, "Yes, that's what I want to do, work with little ones."

During summer break, I met Roy—four years older than I was—a man of the world. He'd spent almost three years as a pilot in the Air Corps. Oh, he could really tell a story. I'd listen to him and dream of traveling away from Minnesota one day. He had an edge about him though, and a kind of arrogance. I thought it was to be expected after the stress of war, and I was certain it would disappear when he re-adjusted to civilian life.

We had an October wedding. My younger sister, your Aunt Elise, stood up with me. I was fairly giddy with excitement. Roy took over his father's hardware store in Eldon, and I went to work with him. I had a knack for organization and for making the displays look nice. Everyone mentioned how appealing the store was, and to his credit, Roy acknowledged my hand in it. He'd say, "Helene has such a sense of style. She's made this the most attractive store on Main Street." And it was true.

But my real contribution was in public relations. I always asked customers what was going on in their lives. And I remembered things— whose daughter was having a baby, who had returned from a trip to Florida, or had family coming to visit. I really cared, and people could tell. Roy was apt to snap at a person who asked for a product we didn't carry, but I would find out why they wanted it. Together we'd decide if something we had in stock might work for them and, if not, I'd make a special order. It all came natural to me.

I got pregnant in January and worked until the beginning of May. Roy didn't think it would be proper for me to work in the store once I started to show. That was a disappointment to me because I wanted to share our good news with the customers who'd become my friends. But I busied myself at home getting ready for you. A neighbor woman taught me to knit, and I made a sweater and booties and a cap. All in yellow of course—right for either a girl or a boy.

You were a good-natured baby. Your smile brought out something nice in people. Even your father showed a tender side with you. When you turned three, I went back to the store during the hours you were in nursery school. Everyone welcomed me and told me how the place hadn't been the same without me.

Then when you were in first grade, I started working full time. I'd go in before the store opened to organize the stock and do the bookkeeping so I could be home with you after school. Once in a while your father would say he appreciated the work I was doing, but more often—right in front of a customer—he'd berate me for the smallest oversight. And he could be so cold. I knew people pitied me for his lack of kindness. It embarrassed me, but I took solace in the customers and, more than anything, in you. Your love filled me with a warmth his coldness couldn't penetrate.

Though he tried to make up for his severity with presents—jewelry, a fur coat—most material things didn't mean much to me. But when you were eight, he surprised me with an idea for a different kind of gift. One Sunday in November he said, "Helene, I know how much you enjoy the morning light. We ought to build you a solarium on the east side of the dining room facing the rose garden." He said we could start drawing a design for the room right away and begin work on it the following spring.

I was so thrilled I couldn't keep the plan to myself. When I told Mrs. Cramer, the first customer in the store the next morning, she said, "You should talk to Wendell Sturtz—you may know him—the handyman. He built a sunroom for his daughter after his wife died. That was years ago, probably before you moved to town. It's a dear little space. He'd be happy to show you."

I did know him. He'd replaced the sash cords in our upstairs windows the previous year. I decided to tell him about our project.

Well, I did just that the following Monday, and he invited me to drop by his home some afternoon. On Thursday of that week, while you were at your Brownie Scout meeting, I walked over to his house. Mrs. Cramer was right, the solarium was like a little gem off his daughter's bedroom. The workmanship was beautiful, and it gave on to the yard in the nicest way.

We got to talking. He was a gentle person, and it was such a pleasure to talk with a man who spoke so politely, who listened to me, that the time just slipped away. Before I knew, it was five o'clock, and the sun had set. Mr. Sturtz insisted on walking me home. "Your mister would never forgive me if I let you walk across town alone in the dark."

Your father met us at the door with a look that scared me, but Mr. Sturtz was oblivious. His tone was so earnest. "Here she is, Mr. Johnson, all safe and sound."

He opened his mouth to say something else, but your father interrupted him. "I've heard more than enough from you." He slammed the door in the poor man's face.

I went to our bedroom and cried until he came in and told me it was out of the question for me to continue working in the store after what had happened, that he simply couldn't trust my judgment. He spat his words at me, "Walking across town in the dark with that low-class man. Disgusting." All our years together, and my innocent interaction with a man had destroyed his trust. "Don't worry about Mary," he said. "I sent her to the neighbors' house after her scout meeting so she didn't hear any of this. We'll make certain she never learns what you've done. Do you understand?"

I didn't understand. I was confused and frightened. When I told him I was ashamed, he gave a curt nod and walked away. I believe he thought I was ashamed of my behavior, but that wasn't it at all. I was ashamed of him, of his cruelty to a man who'd been trying to be kind.

Your father laid out restrictive rules for me and you, and I complied without question. Eventually, I could hardly imagine life being any other way, but sometimes I'd look at you and long for the happiness we used to have. Once in a while I'd remember Mr. Sturtz and wish I had the courage to call him—to apologize for my husband's words. But I'm not courageous, not honorable. An honorable woman would have called him. Would have spoken up to her husband. Wouldn't have disowned her daughter.

I've really rambled on. Probably included too much about my own life. All I meant to do was apologize—to explain why I can't travel to visit you. I make no excuses. After what I've done, I'm not worthy of seeing you again, of meeting your lovely husband and beautiful baby. I hope your life together will be happy. I miss you. I'm not sure I ever said the words, but I've always loved you, Mary. I always will.

◆

Ellie, her face bathed in tears, slid the pages back into the envelope. She wept for her grandmother—the emotionally abused woman who never sent her words of explanation and apology to the daughter she'd rejected—and for her mom, who never got to read them. *My grandmother sat alone in Minnesota, remembering my mom. Trying to imagine me. We never had each other. All that potential love, gone to waste.* But a little cheer made its way up through Ellie's sobs. *My grandmother, fragile though she was, did love my mother. Mom clung to that belief through all the years of rejection, and she was right.*

Ellie had a photo to place on the mantel and a story that would gradually take up residence in her mind and heart and become a part of her. A story she would begin to tell Lizzie. "My grandmother found it difficult to show her love, but she did love her daughter, my mom, your Grandma Mary. And our whole family feels that love." That's all she'd say at first, but Lizzie was a determined truth seeker. The photo would elicit a dozen questions about that grandmother—and that grandfather. *Questions about my whole family, and myself as well. Some will be a joy to answer, others painful, and each response I offer will generate another question. Eventually, she'll read the apology her great-grandmother wrote. The two of us will explore "the web of our life . . . good and ill together."*

RELEARNING
THE PAST

2018

S unrise. The second Saturday in August. Forty-four-year-old Ellie lay taking in the Finger Lakes sky, as she had done all the mornings of her childhood. She still celebrated each day's first light. But London, four thousand miles from this New York farmhouse, was where she'd greeted the dawn for the past ten years.

On Thursday, she and her husband, Will, and their children had flown to New York City and driven north to Tompkins County for their annual summer holiday with Jane and Mark, parents of Andrew and grandparents of Danny, the husband and son Ellie had lost eleven years earlier.

Lizzie, eight years old, and Jack, six, loved spending time on the farm with Mark and Jane, but this year they wanted to investigate Cremona, the town where their mum grew up. Ellie's father and younger brother had died when she was seventeen. When her mom died eight years later, Ellie cut all ties to her hometown. Now as she explored with the children, she might connect some of the loose ends she'd left behind. "Let's walk to the house where you used to live, Mum," Lizzie said.

"I think I showed it to you a few years ago when we came here for lunch with Grandma."

"But we were little then. I don't remember it very well, and Jack was only two or three. He can't remember anything."

They stopped for ice cream on Lake Avenue, turned left on State Street, and walked two blocks. Ellie pointed out a small white house surrounded by a neglected lawn. A forlorn yew hedge hugged the foundation. "You lived in a sad house," Jack said.

A scene awash in the colors of cherry trees and strawberry beds and an ever-changing array of perennials played in her mind. "No. It used to be a happy house."

The next stop was the lakefront site where Ellie had spent her summers. She walked to the porch and greeted a middle-aged woman deadheading geraniums. "Mrs. Evans, I'm Ellie. I called yesterday. You may remember that I came round several years ago."

"Of course, I remember. You were all alone." The woman smiled at Jack and Lizzie. "And now you've brought your children."

"Yes," Jack said, "and we're wearing bathing suits under our clothes so we can swim in the lake." Lizzie gave him a slight poke in the ribs, and he added, "If it's all right with you."

"It will be my pleasure. Go right ahead." She waved toward the water.

The children pulled off sandals, shorts, and shirts and ran down the dock the way Ellie and her brother had done a thousand times. "Mum, you told us the lake was cold," Lizzie yelled, "but it isn't at all." The glinting sun and the sound of her children's voices glancing off the water carried Ellie back to long, glorious summer days. And to the day childhood had ended right here in the flames that took her dad and brother.

Jack's delighted laughter—so like that of the brother and son she had lost—rang out a rich refrain that mingled past and present, sorrow and joy. She remembered the words of her first therapist, *"Closure is overrated. Open every door. Keep relearning the past."* It was a never-ending process.

The Sunday morning plan was for the whole family to visit the Farmers Market. Will bowed out. "I've got a dozen emails to answer and a paper to prepare for the social justice conference in September. You go on. Take the children. I'll make good use of a couple hours alone."

"Remember, summer apples are in," Mark said as Ellie started the car. "You two kids, be on the lookout for them and bring some home."

The lakeside pavilion—with over a hundred vendors of fresh produce, prepared food, and handicrafts—buzzed with talk and laughter. The fragrances of sweet bakery goods and savory breakfast and lunch offerings floated in the air, and the sound of music drifted up from the waterfront. "May we go off on our own?" Lizzie asked. "It'll be more fun that way."

"Okay. You check your watch and meet me right here in thirty minutes. That'll be one forty-five."

Lizzie, always punctual, was waiting at the appointed spot with Jack when Ellie showed up. "Grandpa wants us to buy apples," Jack said. "We found some. Follow me."

He led Ellie to a stand where an attractive woman with dark hair and eyes and stunningly toned arms finished helping a customer and turned to the Bonhams. Lizzie said, "Our grandpa, Mark Campbell, gave us money to buy five pounds of summer apples."

"Mark is your grandfather? You're David's children." Smiling, she looked from one child to the other and then at Ellie. "You're his wife?"

"No," Lizzie burst out, "Uncle David has a wife, but they don't have any children."

Ellie patted her daughter's shoulder and said, "I'm Ellie. I was Andrew's wife, and these are my children, Lizzie and Jack."

The woman took an audible breath. "I'm so sorry—I thought-"

"Of course, I understand how you'd make an assumption. You knew David when he was young?"

"Yes, and Andrew too. Very well. Years ago."

"I met Andrew in London twenty-five years ago; it would have been before that. We lived in Brooklyn when we moved back to New York. I never got to meet any of his old girlfriends. Is that what you were?"

"Hmm . . . kind of . . . but not exactly. I was very fond of Andrew, actually of both him and David, but Andrew was really special." She weighed out the apples and gave Lizzie change for her five dollar bill. "By the way, I'm Jessie. Say hi to Mark and Jane for me."

Back at the farm, Lizzie and Jack ran outside to play fetch with the retriever, and Jane sliced apples and a wedge of local cheddar for the adults. "The woman who sold us the apples was Jessie," Ellie said. "She knew Andrew and David. She wanted me to tell you both hello."

"Oh, yes. Jessie Thorne," said Mark. "I heard that she'd come back with her husband to run the family orchard. Quite an undertaking, but I remember her as a spunky girl. A hard worker."

Jane looked thoughtful. "The summer Andrew went out with her was really something for him. He spent the next five years looking for someone to measure up." She touched Ellie's hand. "He finally found you."

"Really? She was so important in his life and he never mentioned her to me? That's surprising. I thought his past was an open book."

"Andrew never talked to Mark or me about the relationship either, but we could tell it was special. I know uncovering the past is important to you. It might be interesting to talk with Jessie. I'll give you directions to Thornes' Orchard if you'd like. Leave the children here and take a journey back into Andrew's life."

"I'm not sure it would be appropriate for me to seek her out and ask about Andrew. What do you think, Will?"

"Mmm. I know your motivation. Discovering connections between the past and present is an ongoing project for you. Some might call it . . . an obsession." Ellie laughed, and he continued, "It's impossible to know how the woman might react, but I say give it a go. If she's not interested, thank her and buy some apples."

⬥

The next day, Ellie drove to the orchard without calling in advance. *This way, if she doesn't want to talk, she can say she's busy and that will be that.*

She arrived at nine and caught Jessie on the front porch, tugging off her boots. "You're Ellie, aren't you? If you're here for more apples, follow me out to the shop. We've got plenty."

"I will buy some apples, but that's not why I've come round. I told Jane and Mark about our meeting at the market. They both spoke highly of you. I'm a psychotherapist who specializes in dealing with loss. It's taken me a while, but I've learned to be my own patient. Listening to stories about Andrew helps me carry out the everlasting process of grieving. If you have the time and inclination, I'd love to hear some of your memories."

Jessie shot Ellie a quizzical glance. Then with a wave and a cheery voice, she indicated a small wicker table and two chairs under an arbor. "Okay, have a seat." She disappeared into the house and returned carrying a laden tray. "You're the therapist," she said as she sliced an apple strudel and poured two mugs of coffee. "You start."

"Of course. Starting conversations is my specialty. Yesterday when I asked if you'd been Andrew's girlfriend, you said, 'Kind of, not exactly.' Later Jane told me you'd been very special to him. She's perceptive; she knew Andrew as well as anyone did. So I'm wondering what you meant when you said those words. By the way, if you don't wish to answer, feel free to dismiss me, but . . ." Ellie looked at her plate. "I am not about to leave until I finish this strudel."

Jessie glanced across the yard. "Hmm. I knew David first. I had a *kind of, not exactly* relationship with him as well. He took me to his parents' farm a couple of times. Andrew was probably fourteen, a thin beanpole of a boy, watching birds and looking at bugs." She paused, and Ellie waited.

"Two years passed before I actually met him. My mom told me the younger Campbell boy was in the orchard sawing some downed trees and had me carry a jug of lemonade out to him. I expected a version of the skinny kid I'd seen at their farm. Instead, he was this broad-shouldered, golden, Greek god of a man, splitting wood. I was stunned. Some girls might have gotten shy and quiet. That wasn't my style. I flirted with him." She grimaced. "Andrew wasn't having any of it. Just gulped a glass of lemonade and went back to work." Jessie paused again. "My god, should I keep talking?"

"Yes. Until you feel like stopping."

"Later, when I told him I'd slept with David while his real girlfriend was studying abroad, he was disapproving—even after I explained that she and David had agreed to see other people for the summer. His prudishness put me off a little, but the truth was, he'd captured me the day we met when he picked up his splitting maul and said he needed to get back to work. I was my dad's only child. I'd worked side by side with him in the orchard from the time I was eight years old. I had a nonstop work ethic, and I recognized it in Andrew. I wanted to get to know him." She grinned. "Of course, the fact that he was a hunk didn't hurt." She paused and took a drink of coffee.

"Please talk as long as you want," Ellie said. "I'm a good listener."

"Okay, I'm going to try to explain our relationship. I've never talked about this before. Stop me if I start giving more information than you want."

"Don't worry. You won't."

"It was complicated. Andrew was sixteen—an innocent—and at almost nineteen, I considered myself experienced. I was attracted to him, but I thought I should be his protector, his mentor. For a while, we were just friends. We hiked most days until we were too out of breath to talk. Learned what made each other laugh, what we believed in. Then one night he kissed me, and the relationship underwent a major change. It was no longer platonic." She paused again and Ellie nodded. "For two months we carried on a torrid, completely secret affair. It wasn't love. We were friends with benefits long before that term became popular. I wanted Andrew to cherish what we had, then go find a girl his own age—one who wouldn't be a secret—and fall in love. I always hoped I'd succeeded, but I never knew. I went back to school in Colorado at the end of the summer and stayed out there after I graduated. Eventually met the man I'm still married to. I ended up happy, but I never knew what happened to Andrew—until I heard about the accident that took him and your son." She clasped her hands together and looked intently at Ellie. "Did he end up happy?"

"Yes. He was as happy as anyone I've ever known. Patient, totally at ease with life. And curious about everything. An intellectual who carried the Finger Lakes in his heart wherever he went. He and our son spent the day before they died up here on the farm they both loved." Ellie looked at the sky and wiped away her tears. "Jane said Andrew searched five years for someone to measure up to you, and he found me. That's a compliment to both of us, don't you think? . . . It's interesting, though, that Andrew talked about other relationships and never mentioned yours. Never said a word about the connection both you and Jane describe as special."

"Hmm. I told Andrew to hold the memory of our time together in his heart until he met the right girl. You were that girl; he could've told you. I don't know . . . maybe our relationship wasn't so much a story to tell as it was a gift to share."

"Yes, yes. That's what he did. I was a sad girl struggling to grieve the deaths in my family. Looking for love but afraid of finding it. Andrew recognized my need and offered me the gift you gave him. Thank you." She took one last bite and put her fork down.

As she turned to leave, she remembered the apples. "Wait, I had an excuse for coming today. Mark loves those early apples. I want to make him a pie. I'll take a quarter bushel." They walked to the shop, and Jessie filled a wooden basket with the red- and green-streaked fruit. Ellie reached into her pocket. "How much do I owe?"

"There's no charge. I'm celebrating the gratifying answer to a thirty-year-old question."

Ellie turned and walked to her car. *I'm celebrating as well—the affirmation of life's sublime truth. We never really lose those who die before us. They inhabit us, transform us, carry us into the future.*

STARTING OVER

2018

The day after Thanksgiving dawned cold and still. Mark Campbell paced the length and breadth of his Finger Lakes farm, admiring tidy fields prepared for winter and the ragged beauty of the woods silvered by morning frost. He loved it all.

So many Thanksgivings here—sixty-two of them. Yesterday had been one of the quietest. David and Angela had spent the holiday with her parents in California. And Ellie and her family lived in England. They visited every summer—once in a while at Christmas—but a roundtrip transatlantic flight was too much for Thanksgiving weekend.

He and Jane had been alone, but not lonely. They were never lonely when they were together. The day was an anniversary celebration for them. Fifty-two years ago, on their first Thanksgiving together in this house, Jane had asked him to marry her. They laughed as they toasted that day and the lively ones when their boys, David and Andrew, were young. But Mark's favorite Thanksgiving memories were of their grandson Danny, Andrew and Ellie's son. The little boy would come skipping across the lawn on Wednesday afternoon calling, "Grandpa, we finally got here."

He'd leap into my arms, and joy would reign for the rest of the weekend.

Yesterday had been their last Thanksgiving on the farm. They'd sold it to Mike and Lisa, a young couple with two little girls, who wanted to live the kind of life he and Jane had lived their whole married life. Saying goodbye to the place where he'd worked the soil, become a man, raised his sons, would be an arduous process, but it was time to move. *Have to face facts, Jane and I can't muster the energy to keep this big old house alive. Can't do justice to this beautiful piece of land.*

They'd made an offer on a renovated Arts and Crafts house in town. *Older than we are.* Mark laughed. *But in better condition.* It had a master suite on the ground floor and a second story with three bedrooms for when the family visited each summer. Of course, the yard had space for a vegetable garden and a flowerbed. They couldn't give those up. But the scale would be modest.

Mark looked at the faded sign at the end of the lane leading to their house. He was thirteen years old when his dad hung the fresh-cut sugar maple rectangle with Campbell Farm stenciled in green on the front gate of the family's newly purchased property. On that February day in 1956, the sign was purely aspirational. His dad had been a mechanic in the Army Air Corps. When he left the military, he opened a garage. Engines were what he knew best. He knew nothing of agriculture, but he and Mark shared a romantic notion of rural life. The twenty-five neglected acres he'd just bought would be a farm one day. The two of them were sure of it.

That first spring, his dad put him charge of a 20-by-40-foot patch of ground that looked to have been a garden at some point in the past. "See what you can make of it," he said. Mark got in touch with the Cornell Cooperative Extension of Tompkins County, and they helped him plan the plot. He spread compost and rototilled and raked the soil with reverence. Planted onions and potatoes and carrots and peas in rows, put in six tomato plants at one end, and designated the other a pumpkin patch. *I cared more deeply about that garden than anything I'd undertaken in my life.* The harvest was abundant. The family ate all they could, his mom canned a winter's worth of tomatoes, and they gave the surplus away.

The property was ideal for a boy with energy and a passion for growing things. The following year, Mark expanded the garden, more than tripled the number of square feet he planted. He enlisted the help of his brother and sister, and within two years the Campbell farm was yielding enough produce to sell for profit at a roadside stand. Each of the kids started a college fund.

Mark's horticultural endeavors sparked an academic interest, and by the time he finished high school he knew he wanted to study botany. *I was lucky. It all fell together for me. Managing the truck farm on weekends during the school year and full time in the summer.*

His mom and dad moved into town during his last year of graduate school. His siblings had long since lost interest in farming, but agriculture had taken hold of Mark's heart. He bought the farm from his parents and planned his life around it. Teaching plant biology was his profession, but farming was his passion.

He was an assistant professor when he met Jane, an undergraduate in his Plant Biochemistry course. The most ebullient student he'd ever taught. One day after class, she said, "You're exactly the kind of man I want to marry, a plant scientist who loves growing plants."

"Well, we'll have to wait until you graduate for that," he replied. "I can't date a student, let alone marry one."

A year after she graduated, on her twenty-second birthday, they did marry. "This farm needs flowers," Jane said, and set to work clearing a field for a peony bed. The next spring, she put in a second one and planted a quarter acre of lavender.

She'd planned to take a full month off from gardening the year David was born, but there she was—not two weeks after his birth—working in the field with the baby strapped into an infant carrier. "Women have been doing this for eons," she said. Her energy never flagged. She taught high school, cared for the children, and enlarged her gardens until their flowers became the centerpiece of the family's stand at the Farmers Market.

Andrew came along four years after David. The two boys were a study in contrasts. David was a go-getter—outgoing, tall and muscular, as bright as he was athletic. Andrew was tender and contemplative and small for his age. He watched his older brother with bewilderment. Then, when he was seven, he discovered nature—found where he belonged— and never looked back.

Both boys stayed in the Northeast for their undergraduate degrees. They worked on the farm during summers. David, out of a sense of duty. Andrew, for love. After graduation, David left for Caltech to study astrophysics. Jane and Mark couldn't imagine Andrew ever traveling that far afield, but in 1993 he took off for England to complete a postgraduate programme in biochemistry.

Two years away at King's College in London reinforced Andrew's love of the farm. When he finished his course and returned to New York, he vowed he'd never again spend so much time so far from home. He and

Ellie, the girl he'd fallen in love with in England, moved to Brooklyn and spent most weekends on the farm. "My heart's always here, Dad," he said one Saturday morning as they walked through the woods. "Sharing this place with my son is the most important thing I do."

Every year, a couple of weeks before Halloween, Andrew and Danny made a special trip up to the pumpkin patch Mark planted when he was thirteen. It had taken over the entire 20-by-40 plot, grown far beyond it, and become a neighborhood legend. Danny always chose two perfect pumpkins, "humongous ones" he called them, one for himself and one for his grandpa.

With intermingled joy and sorrow, Mark remembered a sunny Tuesday afternoon. Eleven years earlier, but he could still smell the air of that October day. Could see Andrew and Danny, his flesh and his blood. Gathering pumpkins, filling the field with laughter, making the hours rich. And one day later—as they drove home to Ellie—taken in a terrible automobile accident. Gone, but for the memory, from everyone who loved them. Losing them had been unthinkably painful. *Worse for Ellie than it was for Jane and me. We feared she might not survive the loss.*

Time had dulled Mark's stabbing pain, but it never filled the empty space in his heart. *I'm a scientist, a farmer. I'm no poet. I can't call up graceful phrases to express my feelings. Words don't come, just tears.*

Ellie did survive, learned how to carry her husband and son wherever she went, and invited Jane and Mark to share her journey. Memories bound them—the living and the dead—together. *She'll be our daughter for as long as we live.*

He remembered Jane's exclamation, "We've always wanted a daughter," on the June day they first met Ellie at the Ithaca bus station. The girl had looked at Andrew with a question in her eyes. She wasn't used to Jane's effusive way. Even Mark was surprised at the intensity of his wife's outburst, and he'd known her for almost thirty years. It was true though. They had wanted a daughter and they got one in Ellie. She married Andrew, and through her they got Danny, to hold for five years, to love forever.

Mark and Jane's notion of family was expansive. They had two more grandchildren. *Ellie's children, Lizzie and Jack, are ours as surely as if they were of our flesh.* Will, Ellie's new husband, had become their son. *Ah, life is a bountiful mystery.*

Mark pulled off a glove and ran his fingers along the top edge of the weathered sign on the front gate. The new owners wanted him to leave it, wanted to call their home Campbell Farm. They considered the small plot of family graves sacred; they wouldn't touch it. Jane would continue to tend its plantings, and he'd be available by phone and even on site to offer advice throughout their first years as truck farmers. *We're placing the farm in good hands.*

He walked up the garden path toward the front porch. Smelled coffee and bacon and heard Jane's off-key morning song. The two of them would sit at the kitchen table as they had all the mornings of their life together. They'd discuss their plans for the day. Talk about the past, how they'd carry it with them as they left it behind. And make plans for the future.

Maybe we'll take a trip to England. Visit Ellie and Will and the children in London. Stop in Liverpool. Relive our honeymoon. Mark had been a Beatles fan since 1964. Their music had been the soundtrack of his adult life. He hummed John Lennon's "(Just Like) Starting Over" as he opened the door. *Starting over. That's what we're doing. It's going to be good.*

LOVE & THANKS

Friends and family for enthusiastic and perceptive reading.

Cheryl for encouragement and ever-gentle mentoring.

Writers of WYTT for mindful listening and insightful questions.

Bill for unending support, brilliant collaboration, true partnership.